'I wish I could work miracles,' Alex said.

Nicola remembered his mission and tuned in to his mood.

'Think how bereft they would be without you. "The doctor" is not only a tower of strength, but a salvation at a time like this. . .waiting for your car; the sound of your voice; the relief and comfort you give even when the news is grim.'

Their gaze held, as he said, 'Thank you.'

Dear Reader

Caroline Anderson's PERFECT HERO has a shock in store, while Dr Laura Haley is determined to pull Dr Ben Durell out of his refuge in Marion Lennox's THE HEALING HEART. We welcome back Sonia Deane, who tackles the thorny question of doctor/patient integrity, while TOMORROW IS ANOTHER DAY by Hazel Fisher explores the recovery of two people who have been badly hurt in the past. Enjoy!

The Editor

Sonia Deane is a widow with one son, lives in the Cotswolds, and has written a considerable number of books. The Medical Romances were fortuitous. She chose a doctor hero and from then on her readers wanted a medical background. Having personal friends who are doctors enables Sonia Deane's research to be verified. She has also been out with an ambulance team and donned a white coat in a hospital.

Recent title by the same author:

REPEAT PRESCRIPTION

DOCTOR'S TEMPTATION

BY

SONIA DEANE

MILLS & BOON LIMITED
ETON HOUSE 18–24 PARADISE ROAD
RICHMOND SURREY TW9 1SR

All the characters in this book have no existence outside the imagination of the Author, and have no relation whatsoever to anyone bearing the same name or names. They are not even distantly inspired by any individual known or unknown to the Author, and all the incidents are pure invention.

All Rights Reserved. The text of this publication or any part thereof may not be reproduced or transmitted in any form or by any means, electronic or mechanical, including photocopying, recording, storage in an information retrieval system, or otherwise, without the written permission of the publisher.

This book is sold subject to the condition that it shall not, by way of trade or otherwise, be lent, resold, hired out or otherwise circulated without the prior consent of the publisher in any form of binding or cover other than that in which it is published and without a similar condition including this condition being imposed on the subsequent purchaser.

*First published in Great Britain 1992
by Mills & Boon Limited*

© Sonia Deane 1992

*Australian copyright 1992
Philippine copyright 1992
This edition 1992*

ISBN 0 263 77885 1

*Set in 10 on 12 pt Linotron Times
03-9210-48730*

*Typeset in Great Britain by Centracet, Cambridge
Made and printed in Great Britain*

CHAPTER ONE

NURSE NICOLA HARDY lay slightly tense as she awaited the arrival of Dr Alex Moncton. He had been attending her for a virulent attack of flu and she reflected that he was an intriguing character about whom she had learned very little during that time. She found herself studying him outside his profession, as he greeted her.

'This should be my last visit,' he said in a deep attractive voice as he approached the bed.

She smiled and slid out of her lacy blue jacket, aware of the finality.

'Relax,' he murmured with a gentle authority as he put his stethoscope against her firm rounded breast, satisfying himself that the severe attack was over. 'You're fine,' he announced finally, raising his gaze so that their eyes met and held. Hers were deep blue, set wide apart in an oval face framed with shining chestnut hair in which there were golden highlights, emphasised by the June sun. She was twenty-five, vivacious, passionate and challenging, feeling that Dr Moncton was observing her outside the orbit of his profession and, in turn, she was aware of him as a man. A tall attractive man of thirty-three with intense dark grey eyes, strong features and thick dark hair that lay luxuriantly on his fine head, outlining a broad, intelligent brow. He had a magnetic quality, together with an impressive calm and reassurance. Not a man, she thought, to ignore, or easily forget.

In turn he studied Nicola dispassionately, aware of the engagement ring on her finger and wondering about the man she was going to marry.

'Go quietly for the next week,' he said as he put his stethoscope back into his medical bag and clicked down the lid, after which he looked at her as she lay in the double bed with its padded blue satin headboard. The room was large and high-ceilinged and the muted sound of the Cheltenham traffic seemed the only link with reality. 'You've had a bad time. . .a good thing you'd left the hospital in London and not fixed up any new job.'

She nodded her agreement. 'I'm lucky always to have a base here with my parents in Cheltenham,' she commented. 'Besides,' she added a trifle hastily, 'my fiancé, Stuart Lessing, lives here. He's with a finance company and is in France at the moment.' She went on hurriedly, 'I want to get away from hospital life. I'd promised myself a holiday in June, but I didn't plan on spending any part of it in bed with flu. . .you've been very kind, Dr Moncton, to visit me as you have.'

He smiled. 'You and your parents are my silent patients,' he reminded her.

'Yes,' she agreed, 'we've been with you for over a year—since Dr Carruthers died and we transferred from his practice to you—without needing to consult you since.'

He moved out of the sun's rays and she noticed his tall figure in its lightweight grey suit and blue shirt which he wore with a casual air.

'If there should be any problem you've only to ring,' he assured her pleasantly. He had reached the door and his hand was on the knob as he asked, 'Are you being married this year?' He thought, as he spoke, that he didn't know why he asked the question. It struck him that she was the type of girl one would instinctively trust and thought her fiancé was fortunate. She was easy to talk to and he would like to have remained longer to exchange views.

'Christmas,' she said with a smile.

He left with a murmured, 'Goodbye.'

It was, she thought, impossible to gauge his feelings. To her surprise the door opened again and he said, 'I'd like you to put on a pound or two.'

The door closed again, but his presence lingered.

Jan Hardy, Nicola's mother, awaited Dr Moncton and urged him into a spacious, lofty sitting-room of the flat in the colonnaded house in Lansdown Crescent. It had the atmosphere of a drawing-room and was furnished in shades of petunia and jade. But it was a friendly, lived-in room where everyone relaxed. Jan was forty-eight and looked young enough to be Nicola's sister. She wore her hair short and had a faintly scatterbrained air which was endearing. Her face was small and happy, her brown eyes sparkled, yet could be compassionate in times of trouble.

Alex Moncton liked her. She was concerned without fussiness. It struck him, having also met Timothy Hardy, her husband and Nicola's father, that they were a close happy family with freedom being a dominant feature.

Jan said cheerfully, 'She's better, isn't she?'

'Off the list,' he assured her. 'It's been a virulent attack, but she's had a good nurse.'

Jan chuckled. 'A role for which I was not cut out.'

'Then you've made a doubly good job of it.' Alex Moncton didn't grudge the short while he spent with this woman. She had personality, was direct and didn't fuss.

Again she smiled and said lightly, 'I can't offer you a drink, I suppose? What with patients and driving——' She didn't need to finish the sentence.

His answer surprised him.

'True; but perhaps I might call in sometime and avail myself of the pleasure. I'd like to meet your husband again.'

The spontaneous welcome was immediate.

At that moment Nicola joined them, wearing a cream satin housecoat. She looked pale and shaky and was glad to sit down in the nearest armchair. Alex Moncton thought she seemed taller than he had imagined, since he had only seen her while she was in bed. In turn she thought that, talking to her mother, he looked much more vital and animated outside his role as her doctor. She wondered if Stuart would like him.

'Stay up for lunch,' he said to her, 'and then have a rest.' His expression was concerned. 'You'll have had enough by then.'

It struck her that he was a compassionate man who, while never building up the seriousness of her condition, avoided the hearty, 'What you need is a good long walk in the fresh air!'

'I shall be fine in a couple of days when my legs belong to me again,' she assured him.

He held her gaze as he said, 'I'm not in the least afraid you will drag out the convalescence.' It was an implied compliment and faint colour rose in her cheeks. 'And I must be going.' He looked at Jan. 'I'll claim that drink at a later date,' he promised.

When he had gone, Nicola asked, 'What drink?'

Jan told her, adding, 'He's dishy!' She gave a little light laugh. 'If it weren't for my age and Timothy. . .' Her smile broadened capriciously.

'You're incorrigible, Mummy.'

'Better than being dull. . .'

'He won't take you up on that drink.'

'That's where you're wrong,' came the swift reply. 'We're new and he's got on particularly well with Timothy when he's had a moment to chat,' she added.

'Time will prove.' A wave of sick faintness, due solely to weakness, went over Nicola as she spoke. Her expression became one of disgust. 'I feel so stupid,' she admitted.

'You've only just escaped pneumonia. Dr Moncton hasn't called every day because he likes the look of you.'

Nicola laughed. 'Meaning that he would not be easily ensnared.'

'You could say that. . .lunch.'

'Ugh!'

'Lunch,' came the firm reply. 'You look like a plant that hasn't been watered for weeks!'

Nicola managed to laugh. 'I'd look like a clown if I put blusher on my cheeks.'

Jan hated to see evidence of such acute weakness, but she exclaimed, 'Pale and interesting!'

'I must be thoroughly fit when Stuart gets back. I tried to put some "oomph" in my voice when he telephoned the other night and managed to persuade him to ring me over the weekend when I shall be stronger. He's travelling around, so it was convenient. I wish the posts weren't so impossible.'

'Quicker from America than Europe,' Jan agreed.

It was ten days later when Alex Moncton telephoned Jan to know if he could call in that evening and claim the drink. Jan was delighted, as was Timothy. Nicola was surprised. She studied him as he came into the sitting-room, smiling. His air of naturalness and ease reminded her that the last time he had been to the flat it was as her doctor with all the intimacy that embraced. As he talked, he made it seem that he had known them for a considerable length of time, and she appreciated the pleasure on her father's face as they exchanged views. Her father, at fifty-three, an architect, was an excellent conversationalist, youthful and with an infectious sense of humour. Happiness had given him an air of confidence which was unmistakable.

'I'm glad to see you looking better,' Alex Moncton said as he greeted Nicola. His handshake was firm, his eyes met hers with directness. There was a sincerity in his voice as he spoke while studying her.

'Thanks to your ministrations,' she rejoined.

Alex Moncton glanced over to the drinks cabinet where Timothy was standing.

'Just a small one for me. . .whisky. I'm off duty this evening. My partner Allan Forbes is on.'

Jan hastened, 'Your father still practises, Dr Moncton?'

'Yes...and please, the name is Alex... Yes,' he went on, 'my father is a great asset, for although he has reduced his workload considerably since my mother died he's always ready to help me when necessary.'

Timothy served the drinks and they settled in their respective chairs, formality ignored as they discussed local matters, politics, themselves. Nicola listened more than she talked, aware of the power of this man who made it seem that they had all known each other for a long while. She corrected that, supplanting that her *parents* might have known him for a long while. There was a certain reserve as he addressed her, which she put down to the fact that she was engaged.

In truth Alex was asking himself why he had acted upon impulse when Jan Hardy suggested a drink, and felt that he was there slightly under false pretences since his motive was partly business—rather like killing two birds with one stone—and he said a little later, addressing Nicola, 'May I ask what your plans are professionally?'

She stared at him, surprised, as she answered.

'To find something in the medical world, but not hospital life. A stop-gap until I'm married.'

It was the answer for which he had hoped as he said, 'We need a practice nurse. Ours has had to leave at a moment's notice because of her mother's illness.' His tone was businesslike. 'If you are interested perhaps we could arrange an interview at the surgery tomorrow and go into details.'

Nicola didn't hesitate.

'I'd like that. Thank you.'

'Splendid.' He looked relieved, but did not enlarge on the matter except to add, 'Come about eleven.' He flashed a half-apologetic look in Timothy's and Jan's direction. 'My apologies for mixing business with pleasure.'

They murmured their understanding, delighted by the prospect of Nicola working in Cheltenham and being at home for a change. Even though her visits from London had been frequent on Stuart's account, apart from anything else, since he lived in Cheltenham, it would be good to have her company. Nicola had a bedroom, sitting-room and shower in the roomy flat, and complete freedom. But she chose to include her parents in her life because of her devotion to them and their attitude to her. It was an ideal arrangement.

Alex left a little later, having enjoyed the break from work and finding Timothy and Jan congenial companions. He was hopeful that Nicola might prove to be a replacement for Nurse Chalmers, whom he felt would be forced to sacrifice her future work in order to nurse her mother, who had cancer and, widowed, had no one else to care for her. Nurse Hardy should be able to fill the post for some months to come and give them time to find a permanent substitute. She struck him as being eminently sensible and responsible.

When Alex told his father of the possibility, Philip said, 'Rather an impulsive move, isn't it?'

'The matter's urgent,' Alex hastened. 'It will depend on the interview.'

'Oh, I appreciate that, but doubt the wisdom of it.'

Alex frowned.

'I don't know what you mean.'

'Only that she is your patient and there's a question of authority.'

Alex laughed ridiculingly.

'She's going to be married at Christmas and we don't live in an old-fashioned world.' There was good-natured criticism in his attitude. He added frankly, 'All I care about is her efficiency. She isn't the type to be an intrusion, patient or not.' Without realising it he might have been implying that he didn't care if she had two heads, provided she was capable of doing the job.

The following morning Nicola arrived at what was the surgery—the Moncton house in the Park, tree-surrounded and set well back. There was a basement and four floors, large lofty Regency rooms, the ground floor adapted to practice needs, with consulting-rooms, offices and a surgery waiting-room, giving a suggestion of unlimited space. The rest of the house had been converted into three flats in which Alex, his father and Allan Forbes lived respectively.

Nicola had savoured Cheltenham en route. It was a town of trees, lawns and gardens, its imposing Regency houses vying with attractive modern ones, while the wide tree-lined Promenade with its hanging baskets was one of Europe's most beautiful shopping centres. Nicola felt the security of permanence. For the first time since she had started nursing she was really to live there, not just for holidays and off-duty weekends, but as Stuart's wife. She would enjoy all it had to offer, with its continental area behind the Queen's Hotel in the Montpellier and Suffolk quarter, to say nothing of its wide-ranging entertainments by way of theatres, concerts and festivals.

As she went up the wide front steps of the Moncton house and into the reception-room, a bright-faced blonde with laughing eyes came forward, hailing her with a beaming smile.

Nicola cried, amazed, '*Julie*! Julie Warren! *You*! What are you doing here?'

'I'm the receptionist,' Julie explained. 'I've an advantage; I knew you were coming.'

'But why haven't you got in touch?' Nicola asked. 'We haven't seen each other since we were at the Middlesex together.' She laughed ruefully. 'When I left to go to St Vincent's a year ago, we promised to write, but somehow——'

'I know.'

They both looked apologetic. Julie hastened, 'I've only been here a month. . . I wanted a change from nursing. When I discovered you were a patient. . . I was going to ring you and——'

Nicola nodded her understanding. 'Remember the old days?'

'Do I! We had some fun.' Julie's laugh was a throaty chuckle and they looked at each other with pleasure and affection.

Nicola thought that Julie hadn't changed, there was a zest for living in her attitude and she was very attractive in her white coat and wide red belt which emphasised her excellent figure.

'We can't talk now,' Julie said swiftly and with a professional air. 'Dr Alex—he's Dr Alex to everyone—told me to take you straight to him.' She indicated a passage to the left of the wide reception hall and they began to walk towards it.

'Do you know I'm being interviewed for practice nurse?'

Julie's eyes opened wide.

'Why, no! What *fun* if we could work together again. . . I'll see you later and we'll fix a meeting.'

'Very well.' Nicola spoke with enthusiasm and a few minutes later went into a high-ceilinged room with large Regency-paned windows, where Alex sat at an imposing mahogany desk. Would he call her Nicola after his remarks the previous evening? She noticed that her surroundings had the atmosphere of a study, with an old-gold carpet and hangings. A little wave of nervousness went over her.

In turn Alex realised that there was an air of trepidation in her manner, but he smiled in welcome as he got to his feet and greeted her, indicating the patients' chair. He didn't use her Christian name, but he noticed that she looked smart in her navy and white dress, which was right for the occasion. Not fussy or too casual, he thought.

Nicola suddenly relaxed and said with eager enthusiasm, 'An amazing coincidence—your receptionist Julie Warren and I were at the Middlesex together at one time.'

'Really!' He looked pleased. 'She's very popular and splendid at her job.' He held her gaze, his own friendly and yet contemplative. She found herself wondering about him, for he had an intriguing air of inscrutability that she would like to have challenged, but reminded herself that she was there to be considered for a job, not to assess his character, or try to fathom what he was thinking. It had been so different when she had been his patient and it was strange to realise that he knew every detail of her body.

When they were seated, he began, 'Now, Nurse Hardy, how do you think you could cope with being a practice nurse? It is vastly different from hospital life.'

She squared her shoulders.

'I realise that, just as I realise you know nothing about me or my abilities; so the important thing is, do *you* think I should be able to cope?'

He gave her a good mark for the question. He had to admit that he had lost sight of the wider issues as he sought a way out of their present difficulties. He liked her down-to-earth approach and intelligent eyes. He said seriously, 'I want to make sure that you appreciate what is involved.'

'My imagination takes me some of the way.'

'This is a very busy practice and we haven't any margin for error.' His voice was quiet and firm; there was no question of playing down the disadvantages. 'You have been used to responsibility, so that should not be a problem. What is your nursing background? I know you were at the Middlesex——' He drew her gaze to his. 'Did you train there?'

'Yes. I went there straight from school. I was at the college here.'

He was studying her intently and wondering why she had left the Middlesex.

She read his thoughts as she hastened, 'I went to St Vincent's because I wanted to have the experience of a private nursing home. Oh, I worked in the private wing at the Middlesex, but that was not the same, and I had it in mind to go abroad eventually, like my friends.'

Alex thought she would fit well into a life drenched in sun.

He smiled his understanding as he commented, 'But it didn't work out that way?' A shadow crossed his face. 'Things seldom do.'

Faint colour stole into her face.

'In this case, it was Stuart. It was ridiculous for me to be in London and he here.' She added, 'I'd like to know what my duties would be.'

'You'd give immunisations for travelling abroad, ear syringing, routine injections, and of course blood-pressure checks and tests as required. You'll vet the patients and spare our time, so that we can deal with the necessary complaints. It's a responsible job,' he added meaningfully.

'But not to the extent of nursing.' Her dark eyes mirrored enthusiasm and relief. 'Intensive care and all the new treatments...it can be pretty hair-raising at times.'

It struck him that she would nevertheless be cool in an emergency and take practice nursing in her stride. She had the right background and been trained at the highest level.

'You wouldn't have applied for this job had I not been——'

She cut in eagerly, 'While that is true, I'd nevertheless appreciate something a little less hectic, if you think I'd be suitable.' There was a hopeful note in her voice. 'I can give you references,' she added in a businesslike tone.

'Your qualifications are reference in themselves. And I remember you told me that you had your midwifery.' He spoke reassuringly.

She gave a little laugh.

'Oh, yes; I can deal with any emergency in that direction.'

He studied her. 'Your coming here will be a new experience for both of us.'

'Both?' she echoed.

'Yes.' His manner brought a sudden intimacy. 'I've never had a patient working for me before and you have never worked in private practice!'

'That suggests I'm acceptable.' Her gaze met and held his.

'The implication also being that you are prepared to join us?'

'I'd like to, and with Julie working here. . .that is incredible.' Nicola looked happy.

'Splendid!' His smile was faintly indulgent. He liked her enthusiasm. 'When can you start?'

'Immediately.'

'We'd be thankful.'

They discussed terms and settled all the details. She wondered if she would meet his father, or his partner, whose name, she knew, was Allan Forbes; but he did not mention them.

'I'll get Julie to show you round,' he said. 'You, of course, have your own room, next to Mrs Latimer's office. She's our secretary. Her assistant, Ann Merlin, is on holiday.' He looked at her indulgently. 'I hope you will be happy here. . . I wish I could have more time to talk, but——'

Nicola got to her feet.

He came and stood beside her, creating an atmosphere that made her feel welcome as they walked towards the door, and he stood aside to allow her to precede him. 'I'll take you to Julie,' he said as they crossed the wide reception hall where Julie Warren sat in a small but comfortable kiosk viewing everyone who entered. She came forward.

'Your patient is here, Dr Alex.'

He nodded and smiled. 'Take her into my room. . . I hear that you and Nurse Hardy know one another. I'm glad!' He added, 'Nurse Hardy is going to be our practice nurse, so you'll be working together again. Would you show her round?'

Nicola liked his manner and the friendly way he addressed Julie. He turned to retrace his steps, saying to Nicola, 'Could your being ready to work "immediately" mean tomorrow?'

'Yes,' she answered eagerly.

'Oh, excellent. . .goodbye.' He looked at her gratefully, shook her hand, and went back to his room.

Julie reappeared after having attended to the patient.

'Now come and meet Mrs Latimer.' She grinned. 'This is fun.'

Nicola had an impression of space and many more doors as they reached Mrs Latimer's office, which was taken up with her typing desk and filing cabinets, a high-ceilinged narrow room that bristled with efficiency.

'Here we are,' Julie said as she introduced Nicola, having already told Mrs Latimer of their knowing each other.

'You'll never be more welcome,' Betty Latimer said warmly as she and Nicola shook hands. 'As you know, our Nurse Chalmers has had to leave on account of her mother and. . .well——'

'I understand. . . I can stay now if you like—at least to pick up the threads and get to know the hours and case notes.'

'But that would be splendid.'

Betty Latimer was forty-five and had been with Philip Moncton before Alex joined the practice. She was a widow and had one of those round friendly faces, with intense blue eyes and a clear unmade-up skin. A slightly plump figure suited her and gave her an air of homeliness that made everyone with whom she came in contact comfortable in her presence. Her efficiency matched these attributes and she was greatly valued as indispensable by the practice. She held the reins and knew every inch of the route.

'We open at eight-thirty; consultations by appointment—you will find all the details in your room. Come with me.' She led the way next door to a similar room, appointed expertly with all the necessary implements and cabinets for case sheets. The walls were the faintest shade of pink to avoid the spartan hospital look and inspire confidence. A well-worn mushroom carpet completed a friendly picture and a desk stood facing the door.

'Dr Alex doesn't like anything to look grim,' Betty Latimer explained. 'He says there is enough misery associated with medicine, without the surroundings emphasising it. A very humane man, is Dr Alex—like his father.' She added, 'Everyone thinks highly of them

. . .and you'll find Dr Forbes is easy to get on with. A good doctor, too.' It struck her as she spoke that Nicola looked just right. She liked her expression. She seemed happy and eager, and her attitude held a certain enthusiasm. She noticed the engagement ring with apprehension. Would she marry and leave, just when everything seemed settled? Betty Latimer told herself that she had enough to worry about at the moment, without looking into the future. Probably Nurse Hardy intended to continue to work after she was married.

A little later Nicola familiarised herself with her room, finding out where the instruments were kept, sitting at her desk and studying the case notes.

Julie popped in and said, 'How's it going?'

'Nothing like being thrown in at the deep end. . . I shall learn from the patients when I can give a name to them.'

They looked at each other and smiled.

'Your being here,' Nicola said warmly, 'makes all the difference. How about coming to supper tonight? You know my parents and they'll be delighted to see you. I've my own sitting-room. We can have our meal without any bother and then be on our own.' She met Julie's gaze. 'Where do you live?'

'I've a bed-sit near here,' Julie announced brightly. 'I didn't want to take on anything permanent until I'd made sure my job was to my liking. The alternative was an idea to get a job on a liner or cruise ship.'

'Then I hope you like it here,' Nicola said bluntly. 'Can't have you going off just when we've caught up with each other again. My two best friends in

Cheltenham have taken jobs abroad.' She looked a trifle anxious. 'Is this a good practice to work for?'

Julie didn't hesitate.

'Ideal. . . Must get back to my post. What time this evening?'

'Suit yourself,' Nicola said easily. 'Come when you've finished here.' She added quickly, 'Have you a car?'

'A mini.' Julie laughed.

'Only I'd run over and fetch you. . .'

Julie looked back from the door.

'No need. . .see you later.' She gave a broad grin and was gone.

Nicola remained, losing all sense of time. And as she was about to get up from her desk, Alex appeared.

'Mrs Latimer told me I'd find you here.' He looked pleased.

'I wanted to find my way around and feel at home,' she explained.

'A splendid idea, but it's lunchtime.'

'I didn't realise.' She met his gaze. He was studying her with intensity as though summing her up and was in truth telling himself that he felt very lucky to have found someone with such excellent nursing background and who obviously wouldn't be afraid to take authority. He liked Nicola's large frank eyes and her air of confidence, the fact that she was his patient suddenly intruding.

'I feel like Sister sitting in her office,' Nicola said, putting on a haughty air. 'Very much in command.' Her voice was low and she studied him as she added, 'Little did I think, when you first came to see me when I had flu, that I'd be here a matter of weeks later.'

Alex recalled his father's misgivings and dismissed them with greater confidence than he had in truth done originally. A thought struck him disturbingly. So far, Nurse Hardy's fiancé had not been mentioned.

'Is your fiancé likely to object to your coming here?'

Nicola shook her head and gave a little laugh.

'Good heavens, no! He understands my wanting to work. I couldn't be idle for six months.' She paused before adding, 'When it comes to it, I've an idea I shall keep on working after I'm married.'

Sudden silence fell between them and Alex found himself saying almost involuntarily, 'In which case you might consider staying on with us.' A feeling of relief spread over him. His gaze was searching.

'I'm sure I'd love to stay on,' she said eagerly.

Later, they were to remember those words.

Julie arrived at the Hardy flat at six-thirty that evening. Timothy was home and he and Jan welcomed her as though they had seen her yesterday. She thought they were a terrific couple and, even though she had met them on only a few occasions, felt she had known them all her life.

'A happy coincidence, your being with Alex,' Jan said brightly.

Timothy seconded that. He had been concerned at Nicola's isolation from her old friends as they had gone abroad, and missed the happy parties that Nicola used to give when she came home on her off-duty periods.

Nicola never took her parents' attitude for granted, nor her good fortune in having such a harmonious background. A background, she told herself, that she wanted for her children, saddened by the fact that after her birth Jan could not have another child. Nicola would have loved a brother or sister.

Julie took up that theme when she and Nicola were alone in Nicola's sitting-room a little later, having arranged to join Timothy and Jan for supper at eight.

'You are one of the luckiest people I know,' she said as she sipped the white wine they had chosen. 'Your parents are ideal.' She looked around at the comfortable but artistic room. 'And you've privacy as well as companionship and help laid on.'

Nicola's expression was full of appreciation.

'I don't underestimate my good fortune,' she said quietly. 'I'm very very lucky—in every way—and now I've even got what seems to be an ideal job in the circumstances.' She hastened, not wanting to be the subject of conversation to the exclusion of all else, 'How are your parents?'

'In the process of divorce,' Julie replied regretfully. 'They split up some months ago. It was never a happy marriage and it's given me a rather jaundiced view. My father has someone else and they'll marry when he's free. My mother has a would-be lover and it's all very civilised.'

'That, at least, is a bonus,' Nicola suggested. 'But I'm sorry...don't be jaundiced. Think of the masses of happily married people.'

'Thus,' quipped Julie, 'speaks the happily engaged romantic, who also happens to have ideal parents.'

Nicola felt awkward, hating the idea of sounding unsympathetic, or lacking in understanding.

Julie hastened, 'I didn't mean to be self-pitying or grudging you your happiness.'

Nicola didn't know what was the best thing to say and fell back on the safe, 'You'll find the right person——'

Julie's laugh was mocking. 'I thought I had; we lived together for six months, but it was a hopeless failure.'

Nicola looked sorry, but before she could speak Julie put in, her tone changing, 'I'm just being a pain in the neck. . . I don't usually moan and I make the most of my life. But seeing your parents——' she gave a little sigh '—they held up the mirror, as it were. . .'

Nicola thought almost guiltily that she had never known unhappiness; that, thus far, she had led a charmed life, the tide always in her favour.

'We must see what we can do to change the pattern,' she said brightly. 'At least you're working for two bachelors. . . Dr Alex is rather charming—friendly, but there's just something inscrutable about him. Difficult to know what he's thinking.'

Julie's eyebrows raised in faint surprise as she said, 'Well, that is almost inevitable, isn't it?'

Nicola looked surprised.

'I don't see why.'

'You mean,' Julie said, astonished, 'that you don't know?'

Nicola tensed without realising it.

'Know what?'

'That his fiancée jilted him—broke their engagement.'

Nicola gave a little gasp of amazement. She couldn't have explained why she was so staggered by the news of Dr Alex's broken engagement, unless it was because he was the type of man whom one could never imagine being rejected.

'When?' she asked jerkily.

'About six weeks ago—before I started working there.'

And before, Nicola thought, she herself had actually met him.

Julie said in a gossipy voice, 'It was the big topic and I can understand why.'

'He has certainly put on a good face,' Nicola commented, adding, 'What was the reason?'

Julie didn't hesitate.

'Money,' came the blunt reply. 'She ditched him for a tycoon. Older than her. I believe she was quite beautiful. They were to have been married at Christmas, apparently.'

How, thought Nicola, her reference to Christmas must have stung him, and how well he had masked his feelings. Her talk of her own engagement must have rubbed salt into the wound. She felt convinced that he would assume she was unaware of his circumstances, not moving in medical circles, or privy to its gossip. And even had she known, it would obviously not be a subject of conversation unless she chose to mention it.

Julie flashed Nicola a rather surprised look.

'You seem shattered.'

'Just sympathetic. When one is happy oneself. . .and he and I talked today about my being married at Christmas.'

'He's had plenty of practice at concealing his feelings,' Julie said swiftly. 'I think he's been terrific the way he's coped. It must have have been a hell of a blow.' It was a hearty statement. 'But you never know how deep these things go, or if he may not come to the conclusion he's had a lucky escape.'

Nicola nodded. 'Even that wouldn't wipe out the trauma of the experience.'

Julie suddenly looked subdued.

'True; even *agreeing* to part can leave scars.'

Nicola's expression was reflective. She shook her head. 'I can imagine that.'

Julie laughed suddenly.

'Getting solemn won't help. . . I shall meet someone when I least expect it. . . Oh, Nicola, it's good to talk—be together again! Seems like yesterday. I'm dying to meet your fiancé.'

'Stuart.' Nicola glowed. 'You'll get on.'

'And I suppose he's tall, dark and handsome!'

Nicola hastened, 'Tall, dark and with an attractive personality.' There was a note of pride in her voice.

'Sounds intriguing. . . Remember Andrew Carstairs —Dr Carstairs at the Middlesex? He would have been over the moon if you'd agreed to marry him. Smashing, too.' Julie laughed. 'You certainly didn't give him any encouragement, so Stuart must have something pretty special.'

'He has!' Nicola added, 'I met him a year ago.' Happiness danced in her eyes.

Julie sighed. 'Not having a man in one's life is like eating an egg without salt.'

They laughed together and Nicola assured her that she wouldn't be alone for long.

Timothy and Jan received the news of Alex's broken engagement with shock.

'It doesn't seem possible that it could happen to him,' Jan said fervently. 'He would appear to have everything.'

'Except a fortune!' Julie exclaimed drily. 'I hope someone splendid comes along and snaps him up quickly and that he realises he's well rid of dear Karen Templeton.'

Jan seconded that stoutly.

'But he doesn't want anyone on the rebound,' Nicola put in seriously.

When Julie left that evening, the subject of Dr Alex's love life had been thoroughly discussed, as had been the case in numerous homes where his patients were genuinely concerned with his welfare.

CHAPTER TWO

NICOLA settled in and adapted to the practice routine with speedy efficiency. It was very different from hospital life, and she learned to listen to the patients who confided their pet aches, reassuring those who saw in every symptom the shadow of malignancy—even if only having an ear syringed! She also learned how to steer them away from 'seeing the doctor' unnecessarily. In turn, she took a firm stand with those who genuinely needed an examination. She got to know Dr Allan Forbes and liked him. He was an encouraging type, medium height, athletic, with a ready smile and eyes that inspired confidence. He welcomed her with a, 'Thank heaven for Nurse Hardy!' There was a faint pause before he added, 'I never imagined having a patient working for us!' With that he dashed off, leaving a suggestion of vitality. He looked younger than his thirty-four years and was a bachelor.

Dr Moncton Snr was in command, without any suggestion of pulling rank. Nicola thought he was a rather impressive figure, in his late fifties. She knew he came from a long line of Moncton doctors and was a widower who felt the loss of his wife acutely, while masking his loneliness. She could not imagine his ever damping enthusiasm, or spoiling the fun. For his part, he appreciated her bright happy eyes and air of dedication.

Alex went into Nicola's room as she was preparing to go home at the end of her second week.

'How's it gone today?' He thought she looked very attractive in her cornflower-blue uniform with its wide navy belt and a crisp white apron to complete the picture.

'I've had the lot,' she replied naturally. 'Even to a nasty bee sting.' Her smile met his. 'And you?'

'Snap!'

Nicola appreciated how easy he was to work with and had the ability to retain authority while avoiding formality.

They laughed together.

'The joy of the weekend,' she suggested, and then chided herself for her thoughtlessness. Without his former fiancée, surely the prospect must be a little bleak and she did not want to touch a raw nerve.

He said adroitly, 'Your fiancé is home?'

She beamed. 'Coming tomorrow.'

He nodded and seemed to stiffen slightly, as if annoyed with himself for bothering with the question.

'Ah, well,' he said philosophically, 'I shall be kept busy with a midder that's due any time now. . . Glad you've had a good week.' He opened the door, gave a half-smile and was gone. She sat staring at the closed door, feeling sorry for him. No matter how one took it, she thought, a broken engagement couldn't be a pleasant experience. She wondered how deeply his affections were involved, despite the fact that the consensus of opinion seemed to be that he would eventually be grateful.

* * *

It was three weeks later that the whole scene changed and Nicola was summoned to Dr Alex's consulting-room.

She entered apprehensively, tension mounting as he indicated the patients' chair and took his seat at his desk, facing her.

His voice was harsh and there was a grim, critical expression in his eyes as he said, 'I can't find excuses for you any longer, Nurse Hardy. You've been making mistakes, but this one today is inexcusable. You've entered Mrs Lipton's blood-pressure with the diastolic pressure before the systolic——' He thrust forward the case notes which read 90/180, when it should have been the other way round. 'Elementary, but careless in the extreme.' He paused and sighed impatiently. 'I can't fathom what has happened to you. . .you look drawn and vague, and I can't afford the luxury of moods, or tolerate slipshod work a moment longer. Mrs Lipton's case needs careful watching.' His brows puckered, his mouth was drawn into a hard line. Annoyance darkened his eyes. She looked appealingly vulnerable in her uniform and he shot at her without mercy, but with frustration, 'Well? What have you to say?'

For a second there was a heavy silence and then, to his dismay, she burst into tears, hating herself for her weakness as she murmured, 'I'm so sorry. . .but Stuart and I. . .he's broken our engagement.'

Anger drained from Alex in that moment and compassion took its place, the irony of it hitting him forcibly. Emotion, sharp and painful, rushed back; the control he had maintained was threatened by the memory of rejection as Karen had told him that she was going to marry another man—a Ralph Morgan known in Cheltenham as a property tycoon who had a magnificent house on the outskirts of Winchcombe. Thinking of it now, the sting had lessened slightly, but the feeling of wreckage remained, his future plans shattered.

His voice was low and husky as he said, 'I'm *sorry*.' He made an appealing gesture. 'Why didn't you *say*? God knows I can understand and sympathise. . . You know the same thing happened to me.'

Nicola nodded. 'Yes, I know.' She caught her breath on a sob and then calmed herself. 'I wanted to try to carry on normally until I could face things. I only told Julie. I also failed miserably. I can't expect you to overlook my inexcusable mistakes, especially over Mrs Lipton——' She met his gaze with a new appealing courage. 'It was such a shock and——'

'Rejection,' he said quietly. 'The crashing of one's hopes for the future——'

'You felt the same,' she murmured.

'Just the same.' His gaze was gentle; he might have put out his hand and clasped hers, as he added, 'One can retreat into anger on occasions, but in the last analysis one has to accept the inevitable and face the fact that marriage could well have been a disaster.'

'You have great fortitude,' she said admiringly. 'I feel I've been very weak—not a bit the way I imagined I'd be in a crisis. . .also, he was having an affair with someone else whom he's going to marry.'

Dr Alex rapped out, 'You're well rid of him!'

Nicola's gaze dropped to her ringless left hand. She could not see any light at the end of the tunnel. She thought in that second how ironical it was that they now shared the same experience, but it occurred to her that he had come through it with amazing courage. Was it that he already realised he'd had a lucky escape?

Alex again relived the trauma of his own experience, knowing that he had progressed a little after the first crushing blow and that the mercenary nature of the situation gave him a palliative. He did not flatter himself that Karen had had any love for him, but knew that had he, himself, been in the millionaire category she would not have broken the engagement, and that gave him a cynicism which dulled the ache of what he had believed to be his own deep love for her. She had attracted him and he was prepared to admit that her somewhat cool beauty had ensnared him. But with this girl, he suspected, there were no reasons for her loving other than genuine all-pervading emotion that was its concommitant. He did not know why he felt that her suffering was greater than his. The pinched misery of her normally beautiful, vital face told its own tale.

He got up and went to a small cabinet, from which he took a bottle of brandy, and a few seconds later handed her a glass, saying gently, 'This will do you good.' He put a hand on her shoulder, his touch consoling. 'You'll come through it,' he said reassuringly. 'We both shall. The experience is a bond.'

She looked at him gratefully for the much-needed support.

'I'm sorry to have behaved so badly,' she whispered. '*Ashamed.*'

He hastened apologetically, 'And I'm so sorry I took you to task so brutally.'

'You had every right!' Her eyes were unconsciously pleading as she added, 'Could you possibly give me another chance?'

His smile was warm and comforting. There was no hestitation as he said, 'We'd hate to lose you.'

'You've been so *kind*,' she murmured.

They looked at each other and words were not necessary. He broke the momentary silence by saying, his voice deepening, 'Let's hope the future atones for the past.'

She gave a little nod and her soft chestnut hair caught the sun's rays as though a cobweb of gold lay upon it. Recovered a little, she looked very lovely as she sat there, the brandy having brought back a little colour to her cheeks, while the sadness in her large lustrous eyes enhanced their beauty.

'Yes,' she murmured, and lowered her gaze.

'And now I want you to go home.' He added masterfully as she was about to protest, 'And you will obey my order, Nurse.' His voice was deep and held the faintest note of cajolery.

'Yes, Dr Alex.' She capitulated, then, 'Thank you,' she added, 'it has helped—talking to someone who understands.'

There was a tense silence which he broke by saying, 'That's what friendship is all about. . .and now, between ourselves, we can cut out the Doctor-Nurse bit. I'm Alex, as I said when I came to see your parents, Nicola. We've bridged a wide gap in this short while.' His words brought a note of intimacy, stimulated by the use of the word *friendship*.

'We seem to have come a long way since I had flu,' she said simply.

He exclaimed, as though the thought had just struck him, 'I feel for your parents and like them very much!'

Nicola warmed to his words.

'They are very sympathetic. . .and they reciprocate your reactions.'

'I'll look in on them again some time.' He spoke freely.

'They'd like that.' She hastened, 'I'll do as I'm told and have this afternoon off, but I shall be in tomorrow.' Her expression was apologetic and earnest as she added, 'I'm not, I assure you, a crying woman, but knowing I'd justified your anger. . .well, it was too much,' she explained, her voice low.

'And I'm not usually so aggressive,' he replied, 'but I was frustrated as well as angry, Nicola. You'd been so splendid at your job.'

His praise and the sound of her name changed the mood, and she smiled. 'I shan't lay myself open to being "summoned" again, I promise you!'

They looked at each other reflectively. She was touched by his gentleness and general attitude, as well as thankful that no damage had been done to their association. She liked his, 'That's what friendship is all about.' It seemed to set a seal on their relationship, so that she could relax in his presence.

The intercom went. His next patient had arrived.

Nicola got to her feet and he came round from his desk to stand beside her, looking down at her intently. 'You know how I feel. . .the word "sorry" is always so inadequate.'

She managed to sound bright as she commented, 'You *understand*—that is everything.'

A look of gentle contemplation came into his eyes. He found it difficult to imagine any man being unfaithful to this normally vital, appealing girl. His sympathy went deep, but he knew from bitter experience that mere words were inadequate and the wound would not heal with the aid of platitudes. The urge to comfort her was great.

He said, identifying himself with her, 'We shall overcome all this and, as you say, understanding is everything.' His expression was full of concern as he walked with her to the door and opened it. His gaze consoled her.

'Thank you,' she murmured as she left him, feeling that he had become her friend, with whom she could relax and share her own shattering experience.

No one could gauge the depth of the disillusionment they shared, but it was like a hand held out to her in the darkness as he finally said gently, 'Look after yourself.'

Emotion churned within her as she drove the short distance from the Park to Lansdown Crescent and relived the scene where Stuart, instead of taking her in his arms when he came back from France, he said weakly, 'I've something to say and I don't know how to say it. . .you see, I'm breaking our engagement and hate hurting you.' She remembered how he had avoided her eyes and seemed totally inadequate as he hastened, 'I've been trying to tell you, write to you, but——'

Nicola recalled the sick sensation of disillusionment

as she had helped him out. 'Meaning there's someone else?'

He had looked awkward and embarrassed as he said, 'I'm in love with her.' The admission was in the nature of an excuse.

And in that second the name Sarah Robertson had insinuated itself in Nicola's mind. She had heard it on his lips on several occasions, as well as on those of her friends. She flashed, 'And you've been having an affair——'

'I—I. . .well, yes; but I want to marry her.' It had been a defensive admission.

'You could have told me in the beginning.' Nicola could hear the echo of her broken voice and feel again the undermining of her confidence, the emotional turmoil.

'I was a coward.' He had looked powerless as he stood there, without authority.

Nicola experienced again that empty, bereft feeling which had swept over her as she managed to maintain control and slowly, deliberately had taken the ring off her finger and handed it to him.

He had begun falteringly, 'Listen, Nicola; this is the only way.'

'Of course.' A trace of cynicism had given her courage.

He had grasped at that, put the ring in his pocket and, thankful to have escaped a scene, murmured, 'I'm sorry,' and went hurriedly from the room.

The room, and her life, had seemed suddenly empty.

Nicola thought now, as she went into the flat, that she had gone through that ordeal without crying and yet had broken down in front of Alex, the knowledge of her own mistakes, together with his justifiable anger defeating her.

Jan listened sympathetically as Nicola explained why she was home early and confided all that had happened, ending with, 'No one could have been more kind than Alex; he talked of his own feelings and there was no strangeness. He was concerned for you and is coming to see you both.'

Jan's voice was strong. 'Alex is a man of integrity—staunch, reliable.' The words were uttered slowly and with deep sincerity.

Nicola exclaimed bitterly, 'I thought that of Stuart! He could have told me in the beginning. It isn't a crime to break an engagement, but to have an affair, *pretend*——'

The silence was deep and a little uncomfortable before Nicola shot at her mother, 'Did *you* have any doubts about him?' She paused before hastening, 'Come to think of it, you never said very much.'

'The only thing that mattered was your happiness.' Jan did not want to admit at this stage that neither she nor Timothy had trusted Stuart, having doubts about his fidelity and business methods.

Nicola accepted that.

'My coming back to Cheltenham for good,' Nicola reflected. 'The name Sarah Robertson crept into the picture, but I never *dreamed*. . .'

'The wife, or fiancée, is the last to know,' Jan said sagely.

'The numerous weekends. . .so many things,' Nicola said with spirit.

Jan looked at her with gentleness. 'You've had a lucky escape.'

Nicola exclaimed fiercely, 'Why can't one turn love off like a tap? Disillusionment isn't an antidote.'

Jan assured her, '*Time*——'

Nicola couldn't help the cynicism that crept into her voice, 'The cliché that time is some mystical balm and all you need is to find another man!' She made a little explosive sound, then, 'Oh, I like men and I'm not going into a nunnery, but they'd better not start talking about love, or I'll explode!' Her eyes gleamed with a strange fire, giving her a belligerent expression, while her ringless left hand bore testimony to the devastating fact that her life was in chaos, her emotions and hopes shattered.

Jan accepted the outburst. Anger was better than tears; not that Nicola had shed any thus far in her presence. She had seemed stunned and disorientated, talking fitfully and looking drawn. It struck Jan that Alex would be a good influence and she was grateful that Nicola was working for him.

A disturbing thought shot through her mind which prompted her to say, 'Will you stay here in Cheltenham after you leave Alex?'

It was typical, Nicola thought, that her mother posed the question without prompting any advisory answer. She didn't hesitate as she said, 'Oh, yes; and I may not leave him.' She explained the situation, adding, 'I love being here with you and Daddy and, apart from this lapse, I love my job. I'm in no mood to start off round the world. I thought Stuart and I were going to dig some roots. . .' She paused before adding defiantly,

'Well, I'll dig them—alone.' Her eyes gleamed with the fire of determination.

Jan smiled encouragingly. 'You know we love having you here.'

Nicola said warmly, 'You're such splendid parents—real *friends*, and you've allowed me to feel that my rooms are completely mine where I can do as I like and entertain whom I like.'

'Freedom is the one gift we can offer you,' came the swift reply. 'It will do you good to take stock for a while.' She added lightly, 'What is Dr Forbes like?'

She knew, the moment she had uttered the words, that she had made a *faux pas*.

Nicola flashed, 'Just part of the team.' The point being that she was not interested in him and didn't see him outside the role as a partner in the practice.

Jan hastily changed the subject. It was like treading on eggshells.

Nicola took herself to task during the rest of the day, telling herself that if she had any pride she would set her shoulders back and face the future with courage devoid of bitterness. The shock was over and it was useless telling herself that if she had not returned to Cheltenham things might have been different. She was not the first woman to be deceived and it was up to her to face the fact with stoicism.

Thus she arrived for work the following morning, greeting Betty and Julie with a cheerful, 'Sorry I've been such a sick headache lately. . . I'm sane again now.' She gave a little, rather uncertain laugh.

Alex came into her room as she was settling in.

'Ah,' he said, 'you look better!'

He stood before her reassuringly, his expression confident. He brought an air of optimism with him that enhanced his natural attractiveness.

'I gave myself a good talking-to,' she admitted, looking him straight in the eyes. 'Thank you for being so generous. I'm terribly sorry to have fallen down on the job, but being taken to task brought everything to a head and was what I deserved.' She looked appealingly apologetic.

Alex relived the anger he had felt. It took a great deal to rouse him and he didn't deceive himself that the primary reason for his reaction was bound up with a sense of loss because he had congratulated himself on having found an ideal nurse. Both his father and Allan shared his sentiments.

'There are some things one has to face head-on!' he exclaimed, adding, 'Before any adjustment can be made.'

'How true.' There was a trace of defiance in the utterance. 'And I don't underestimate how fortunate I am to be given another chance.' Her mood changed; her voice was warm and soft.

He made a little expressive gesture and his gaze held hers for a second. She reflected that he was the type of man to be a tower of strength in an emergency, and bleakness crept back like a cloud over the sun. Depression was always there just beneath the surface. It didn't seem possible that Stuart had betrayed her and the engagement had been a mockery. A shadow went over her face and the fact didn't escape him.

'Let's hope we have a reasonable day,' he murmured, trying to infuse a note of lightness into his voice that might lift her spirits. 'And don't forget that if there are any problems we are here.'

She countered seriously, 'I am supposed to spare *you* problems.'

He studied her, aware of the changing expressions that passed over her face and how even a half-smile transformed her. Had she been wearing a *haute couture* dress, he thought, she could not look more attractive than in her nurse's uniform.

He lingered for a few more seconds and then left as surgery began.

Nicola's first patient was a Mrs Stevens, who came in half apologetically, not wanting to 'worry Dr Alex'. She was tall and slim, about thirty, with thick blonde hair framing an attractive oval face. Her eyes were large, apprehensive and very blue. She sat down gratefully and winced as she did so.

'I have painful periods,' she said in a breath, 'but this is different.'

Nicola studied her with a trained eye, not liking what she saw.

'Let me take your temperature.'

The reaction was immediate and desperate. 'I'm not ill. . . I can't be ill. I've a son of two-and-a-half and a daughter of six months; a neighbour is looking after them for me. My husband works for the DSS. . .'

Nicola put a thermometer in the patient's mouth and waited. Her temperature was 102 degrees.

'You've pain around the umbilicus—the tummy button,' Nicola hastened. 'And you feel sick. . . I'm going to get Dr Alex to go over you,' she said with a gentle firmness. It was an instinctive decision, and when she picked up the telephone and heard Alex's voice she said swiftly, 'Mrs Stevens needs to be seen immediately. I know I'm exceeding——'

Alex broke in, 'I've a patient just leaving and I'll fit Mrs Stevens in next. . .give me a couple of minutes.'

Nicola was relieved.

At that moment Mrs Stevens, white and distressed, cried, 'Oh! *Nurse*. . .sick.'

Nicola snatched a receiving bowl which was always in readiness in cases of emergency, and got it there in time. The spasm over, they went into Alex's counsulting-room. At the sight of the familiar and obviously ill patient, Alex's brows raised and his eyes betrayed immediate concern.

Once on the examining couch, he went over her quickly and knew they were dealing with appendicitis with the danger of perforation. It was a case for prompt surgery.

While Alex spoke to a colleague who was a surgeon and consultant at Cheltenham General Hospital and arrangements were made for Mrs Stevens to be admitted, Nicola alerted an ambulance.

Mrs Stevens whispered through the miasma of pain and illness, 'The children. . .my husband. My mother would. . .help.'

Nicola put a hand on hers, looking down at the prostrate figure. 'I have your address and telephone number. I'll get in touch. . .leave everything to me.'

Within a very short while Mrs Stevens was on the operating table. A life had been saved.

Alex talked to Nicola at the end of the day when the drama was over.

'But for your prompt action,' he said approvingly, 'there could have been a tragedy. . . Good work.'

Alex felt a sensation of relief. His confidence in her had more than been restored and he felt secure in the knowledge that she would live up to his original expectations, being very much part of the scene. He liked seeing her around and was sensitive to her moods and expressions. She had initiative and he found their brief conversations between patients stimulating, while ever conscious of her moments of depression to which he had become attuned.

He looked at her appreciatively, 'I should say you have a good diagnostic sense.'

'Thank you. . . Oh! I dealt with the domestic situation and traced the husband. The neighbour was most helpful and there is the hope that Mrs Stevens's mother will take over. She is a widow and lives near by at Leckhampton.'

'Oh, splendid.' He looked pleased.

Nicola felt she had taken a step towards redeeming her previous mistakes and a little bubble of happiness touched her, dulling the ache of disillusionment and the memory of Stuart.

Alex's father joined them at that moment and, studying him, Nicola thought he had the dignity of a doctor of the old school. He would, she realised, have known of her defects, but there was nothing critical in his manner to highlight the fact.

'Quite a day, I understand,' he said, his voice deep. She felt the aura of loneliness about him, despite his vital manner. It was two years since he had lost his wife after celebrating their thirty-sixth wedding anniversary.

It had been a swift and dramatic case of overian cancer. 'You have a bonus with Mrs Stevens. . . My patient, Harvey Wilton, didn't make it.'

'Coronary?' Alex spoke quietly. They knew Harvey Wilton well.

'Yes; his second. As you know, he was my age.'

Alex sighed. 'Fifty-seven,' he said in a breath.

'Oh! *Young*.' Nicola's reaction was spontaneous.

A trace of a smile touched Dr Moncton's lips. 'Thank you, Nurse!' He looked from her to Alex. 'How about having a drink with me? I don't particularly welcome my own company at the moment.' There was no self-pity in his voice, just a quiet statement of fact.

Nicola instinctively met Alex's gaze as though questioning his reaction.

'Just what the doctor ordered,' he said without hesitation. 'Or have you a previous engagement, Nicola?'

The 'Nicola' didn't escape Dr Moncton's notice. He found that he liked her.

'No,' she hastened. 'Thank you.' She smiled as she spoke; that illuminating smile which lit up her face and seemed to touch the others with its magic.

The three of them went into the main sitting-room with its large Regency windows and window-boxes that were a mass of colour in the evening light. Shades of blue and gold dominated the décor and well-loved antiques, set at just the right angles, merged with deep armchairs and a large sofa, beside which a coffee-table housed well-thumbed books. The room had retained its feminine touch, for Philip Moncton insisted that everything was left just as his wife, Valerie, had arranged it.

Nicola sank down and relaxed. Her position seemed

suddenly secure, which was very important. To have emotional conflict in her private life and chaos in her professional was nerve-racking. But it was strange to be there, facing these two men, without Stuart; no longer the girl about to be married, but the girl alone. How did Alex feel about his position? She looked at him as he poured her sherry from a decanter which threw off prisms of light and colour from the cut glass. He was quick, and yet managed to convey an atmosphere of leisure as though the moments were meant to be savoured, and as he put her glass down on the small side-table he looked at her with an expression of welcome that made her feel at home. His kindness to her gave her confidence, and she recognised the fact that his attitude that day stimulated her professional interest, investing her job with new meaning and increasing her determination to give it all the skill of which she was capable and thus live up to his expectations.

In turn he felt eminently satisfied that his original assessment of her capabilities had been proved right. He found himself wondering what she was thinking as she sat there and if the hurt of her recent experience lay just behind her smile. From his own case he knew that rejection cut deeply into self-esteem, no matter how one might realise that one had been spared greater suffering.

'I telephoned the hospital,' he said a few minutes later when they were sipping their drinks. 'Mrs Stevens is asleep and all's well.'

Nicola cried, 'Oh! I'm so glad. . .you'd already spoken to Mr Jayson when the operation was over.'

'Oh, yes. Ronald is a good friend of mine. Fine surgeon. You'll meet him later on,' he added as though it were a foregone conclusion.

'Yes,' Dr Moncton put in easily, 'he pops in from time to time. His wife and mine were great friends. Ronald cares about people and that makes his skill doubly valuable.'

Nicola thought the same thing might have been said of Alex and that it was a fine attribute, particularly in the medical profession.

An hour passed, although Nicola had only the one small sherry because she was driving home. Conversation didn't flag and she felt completely at ease. It struck her that she and Alex could be relaxed in each other's company because of a shared experience which negated desire, or even the thought of emotion. They might have been bandaging each other's wounds by virtue of silent understanding; an understanding made possible by the explosive scene of yesterday.

Alex looked at his watch.

'I've a terminal lung case to see before supper. . . The wife has done the nursing until she's on the point of collapse, but he dreads hospital and she's promised him he won't have to go. It won't be very much longer.' There was a prophetic air about him as he spoke.

'The relatives need the doctor as much as the patients,' Dr Moncton said quietly.

Alex nodded.

Nicola's gaze was upon Dr Moncton's face as he said quietly, 'I always have the consolation that Valerie's case was not protracted.'

A sigh escaped Alex, his expression saddened.

'Do you miss hospital life?' Dr Moncton asked Nicola with interest a few seconds later.

Nicola knew that while Stuart was in the picture it was rarely that she had done so. Now it was different and she felt more isolated.

She said tentatively, 'It depends on my mood. . . Not while I'm here,' she added swiftly, and got to her feet. 'I must be going. It's been very pleasant. . .thank you.' She looked from face to face.

'The pleasure has been ours,' Dr Moncton said as he moved towards her and held out his hand. The thought flashed through his mind that she was the last person he could imagine being let down. He had felt the same about Alex, but then Alex was his son.

Alex and Nicola walked down the wide staircase to the main hall. She said sincerely, 'Your father is a charming man. Talking to him outside the restrictions of practice association makes all the difference.'

Alex echoed the word 'restrictions' with surprise, adding, 'I didn't think there were any.'

Nicola hastened, 'None that is obvious, but from the practice nurse point of view a certain restraint is inevitable. Deference. Although your father treats everyone with the same courtesy.' She turned her head and looked directly into Alex's eyes. 'As you do.'

He gave a little infectious laugh.

'I treat all my patients with respect,' he reminded her. 'It is a special relationship.'

She started, having overlooked that aspect. 'Ah!' she murmured. 'I suppose that's right—at least if you often need your doctor.'

'Which you certainly haven't done.'

She shook her head, but just for a second the memory of his looking after her lay between them.

When they went out of the front door and were about to part, his expression changed. He looked sombre.

'I wish I could work miracles,' he said with a heavy sigh.

She remembered his mission and tuned in to his mood.

'Think how bereft they would be without you. "The doctor" is not only a tower of strength, but a salvation at a time like this. . .waiting for your car; the sound of your voice; the relief and comfort you give even when the news is grim.'

'Thank you.' Their gaze held.

He saw her into her car, got into his own and drove away.

Nicola concentrated on her job to the exclusion of everything else during the following weeks, becoming doubly popular with the patients and invaluable to the doctors. Giving satisfaction and being appreciated represented a strange remote kind of happiness, based on a conception that, if your heart was not aching to a point of abject misery, then you were 'happy'. The irony of the concept did not elude her, but she accepted it with stoicism and did her utmost to shut out thoughts of Stuart and the past, without having any idea of what she wanted for the future. One thing she was adamant about: she would not seek solace elsewhere, and refused invitations that might lead to any kind of emotional involvement.

Julie said bluntly, 'You're going about this in the

wrong way, Nicola. Becoming a hermit won't solve anything and engagements are broken every day.'

Nicola didn't like the implication of the words.

'I'm not such a nitwit, and realise that. I suppose it's absurd, but I should have felt more sympathetic towards Stuart if he had told me he was in love with the woman before he slept with her.' She made a gesture of disgust. 'There was I, thinking of years of fidelity and the ideal marriage—*fooling* myself. I'm not likely to invite another man to treat me the same way. No, thank you!' she added emphatically.

Alex during that time felt that he could best help her by discussing and drawing her into his own professional problems. He was aware of the emptiness behind her smile, and the depression manifested by a sudden sigh. He had visited Timothy and Jan on two occasions and had a rapport with them which he valued. He felt instinctively that they were not depressed by the breaking of the engagement and that Stuart had not measured up to their standards. Their unhappiness was involved only so far as the situation affected Nicola. He found that his own experience and the suffering it entailed made him curiously protective towards Nicola, wanting to help her and steer her into a happier path.

Allan Forbes came into the picture at this time. He had become friendly with the physiotherapist, Rosie Gilliat, to whom the practice sent its patients, and had lost his disinterested bachelor air. Alex was pleased; a married partner would be good for the practice, as he had believed his own marriage would have been. He was also pleased that Nicola and Rosie had become friends. He liked Rosie—brown-eyed, dark-haired, outgoing natural type of twenty-five, with a ready wit and mind of her own.

Alex mentioned Allan and Rosie to Nicola as surgery ended after a particularly hectic week and they met in the common-room.

'Of course you're going to their drinks party tomorrow evening?' He was prepared for a negative answer and told himself that he would use all his powers of persuasion to reverse the decision in that case.

To his satisfaction she said, 'Yes; of course. Betty and Julie are going, too.'

Alex had a sudden impulse as he looked at her in the second of silence that followed her affirmation.

'In that case, how about your coming with me? We could have a meal out somewhere afterwards.'

CHAPTER THREE

NICOLA heard the invitation and felt a sudden trepidation, instinctively wanting to refuse. As the silence lengthened, she argued that since she and Alex were in the same boat there was no question of misunderstanding, nor any significance attached to the arrangement.

'Why not?' she said coolly, but with a faint smile. 'Thank you.' She was wrestling with disturbing thoughts that suddenly assailed her. 'Do you think it will turn out to be an engagement party?' She spoke a trifle apprehensively.

He replied lightly, 'It hadn't occurred to me.' There was a faint challenge in his voice as he added, 'Does it matter?' No doubt, he thought, Stuart was on her mind.

A little colour stole into her cheeks and she avoided his gaze as she said, 'No, of course not; but it would be ironical.' She paused before adding deliberately, 'For both of us.' And now she looked at him boldly.

He shrugged his shoulders and commented, 'One cannot live in the past.'

She drank the remainder of her coffee. 'Neither can one pretend it doesn't exist.'

Alex tried to convince himself that he had come to terms with the situation and shut Karen from his thoughts, maintaining that to dwell on the past could wreck the future. He had found that sharing the experience with Nicola had been a panacea, while endeavouring to help her through the trauma had given him a purpose. The suggestion that he and she should go together to the party had been made on impulse and the belief that she would be feeling the isolation of her position, as he was, despite his philosophy.

He echoed her word, 'Ironical,' adding, 'yet the pattern changes, as ours will change. At the moment we are rather like the pieces of a jigsaw puzzle without a picture.'

She accepted that, aware of his wisdom, but such was her mood that she would like to have challenged him nevertheless.

'I'll pick you up at six-thirty,' he said a few seconds later. 'Father will take any calls and contact me in an emergency.' He studied her intently. 'You like Rosie?'

'Very much. Even in this short while we have become friends. I'm glad she is openly in the picture. Allan is a delightful character. I must admit that I'd regarded him as a contented bachelor.'

'Ah!' Alex spoke with feeling. 'There is a wide gap between assessment and truth. Rosie would certainly fit into the picture should they be serious.'

'Yes.' Nicola tried to suppress a sigh, but failed. It seemed so foreign to her to be a woman alone. In normal circumstances Stuart would have been taking her to the party on Saturday. The fact that Alex was doing so didn't bring any solace, while she in no way underestimated the help he had been to her, or the fact that he had carved a niche in her life that was completely outside all sexual stimulus. She could not imagine herself ever being intimately involved with a man again, or trusting one when it came to any emotional tie.

The following evening Nicola bathed and dressed without enthusiasm.

'If I could get out of going, I would,' she said to Jan in a low flat voice. 'Oh, I like them both, but I don't feel in the mood.'

Jan studied her. She looked beautiful in her long powder-blue stiff silk skirt and lacy white blouse, which moulded her figure and tucked into a silver kid belt, emphasising her small waist. Her face was touched with the lightest make-up and her skin had a magnolia smoothness, while her eyes, wide, lustrous and appealing, completed a picture of cameo-like appeal.

Jan didn't remind her that she had got into the habit of using that phrase and it was time she stopped; neither did she remind her of the irritating cliché: 'You'll enjoy it when you get there'. In fact she decided to be blunt.

'Stuart isn't worth it, you know.' Jan looked at her long and hard.

Nicola tensed and retorted, eyes flashing, 'I'm aware of that and you're quite wrong if you think he's responsible for how I feel. . .' She floundered because the words didn't ring true. 'It's that one is so alone. The whole pattern has changed. . . Oh, I know Alex has been kind and helped me enormously. But life hasn't any "look forward to",' she said, and the childish phraseology was touching. 'I'm standing outside myself all the time.' She hastened, hating even the possibility of self-pity, 'Anger's gone and I suppose it was a crutch.' She gave a deep sigh, squared her shoulders and added, 'And that's the last time I let the situation get under my skin and make myself sound like a weak fool. Sorry, Jan.'

'Don't be silly,' Jan said practically. 'You wouldn't be human if you didn't have these moments. The important thing is to get back into the swing of life and begin to enjoy yourself again.'

Nicola brightened. 'I know you're right. At least with Alex there is a fellow feeling and I haven't to be on my guard.'

The doorbell rang.

'That will be him,' Nicola said.

'I'll answer it.' Jan moved out of Nicola's bedroom where they had been talking.

Alex came into the flat with an easy familiarity.

'I've got a taxi,' he explained to Jan. 'Everything has been allowed for practicewise——'

'And,' Jan put in cheerfully, 'you want to be free to have a drink or two without worrying.'

He smiled. Jan, he thought, even in that second, was a person who captured one's mood and brought enthusiasm to every meeting. He looked at her, his gaze significant, 'It will do Nicola good to——'

Nicola heard his words as she appeared in the hallway and stiffened as she said archly, 'You make me sound as though I'm a child who needs a toy!' The words rushed out because she had the impression that he was doing her a favour by taking her out and it spurred her to anger and annoyance.

Alex gave her a cool appraisal. He didn't pander to her mood.

'And do you need a toy?' he asked, meeting her gaze with one of challenge.

It wasn't what she had expected and she flushed slightly. She asked herself if she should retreat or attack.

Jan stood there, slightly alarmed by Nicola's expression.

'Since life is a pantomime, it might be just what the doctor ordered!'

Alex ignored that but told her about the car, which she thought seemed to build up the occasion in a manner that didn't appeal to her. She said immediately to Jan, 'I shan't be late...' She moved towards Alex and the front door as she spoke, and her smile was strained. She didn't quite know why she was so furious at the idea of Alex treating her as though *he* knew what was good for her and she was some rather pathetic thing like a bird with a broken wing. She had appreciated his kindness and understanding, but had accepted it as representing a fellow feeling since he was in the same boat. She did not now want to have to think along the lines of his doing her a favour out of pity.

She got into the car almost reluctantly, taking note of his smart dark grey suit and immaculate appearance, but at that moment she had nothing to say to him and silence fell; a silence of which he was acutely aware, yet had no intention of breaking by uttering banalities. The thought streaked through his mind that it was obvious he was a poor substitute for Stuart and he was at a loss to understand why, even so, her mood should be so antagonistic. But he had no intention of pandering to it.

In turn Nicola felt a strange kind of panic, mingled with depression, and as her anger died a little she felt inadequate and was afraid he would find her dull. It was different being *out* with him, identified, and quite another matter. Her hands were clasped tightly in her lap and she tried to think of something to say, perversely willing him to speak.

He did so, briefly and to the point.

'We don't have to make conversation. It is a great thing to achieve companionable silence. I'm afraid my bringing you here wasn't a good idea.'

Nicola felt suddenly mean and incapable of putting on an act.

'I'm sure your motives were noble.' She flashed him a disquieting look.

'"Noble",' he echoed. 'You have a strange choice of words tonight.' His gaze was warning. 'May I suggest that you don't allow imagination to run riot, or give the past a magic it probably didn't possess?'

At that she bristled. 'You can't denigrate a relationship to a point where it lacked all happiness.' Her voice was sharp and almost accusing. 'At least, I can't, even if you conveniently can.'

'That's better,' he said coolly. 'I prefer your anger to innuendo.'

She flushed. 'I'm not angry,' she protested vigorously.

'Then you are a very good mimic!'

She calmed down, furious that she couldn't keep better control of her emotions. The memory of bursting into tears in front of him suddenly crept back, making her squirm. She had never given way before in her life and now, she argued, here she was betraying herself like an upset child.

He contemplated her questioningly, trying to understand her attitude while attributing her mood to the loss of Stuart and telling himself finally that he, himself, had become the whipping boy, amazed at his ability to keep calm.

'In the end,' he said unexpectedly, 'we come back to friendship.'

His words struck the right note and she brightened, 'It is a comforting word. No complications.'

'Or judgements.' He paused. 'Now suppose we pay our host and hostess the compliment of getting in the party spirit?'

There was a note of compromise in her voice as she agreed.

Rosie had a flat near Montpellier Gardens, the town's continental quarter at the top end of the Promenade and conveniently behind the Queen's Hotel, and Mrs Spicer, Rosie's much valued daily-cum-factotum, let Alex and Nicola in. Rosie shared the flat with her unmarried brother, who was visiting their parents in Singapore, the father being in the Foreign Office. It was spacious and on the second floor of a large Victorian house. Rosie didn't mind it having a bachelor air about it, the sitting-room resembling a study, one wall lined with books. Deep ruby upholstered armchairs and a solid mahogany desk gave an atmosphere of permanence and the large windows allowed the late August sun to pour in and send shafts of light upon the scene. The hum of voices and laughter heralded success.

Allan and Rosie came forward, smiling broadly in welcome, while a hired waiter held out the drinks tray.

Rosie Gilliat was an unusual type, colt-like, with

straight shining brown hair that fell loosely about her eager unmade-up face, with its smooth skin and natural colour that gave her cheeks the glow of someone who had been for a long walk on a crisp winter's day. She radiated happiness and the ease which came from an uncomplicated, warm-hearted personality. Nicola felt better the moment she saw her, and relaxed for the first time. There had been an instant rapport between them when they first met and Nicola felt that she could confide in her at any level, knowing she would understand.

In turn Rosie felt drawn to Nicola and was deeply sympathetic.

'I'm so glad you're here,' she said, her voice bright and with an attractive lilt. She looked from Nicola to Alex and gave him an appreciative smile. She liked him and admired him professionally, happy in the knowledge that he had sufficient faith in her abilities to recommend her to his patients.

Allan stood contentedly by, at one with the world.

Nicola searched for a familiar face but was unable to find one, apart from Betty and Julie, who already knew that she was coming with Alex.

When Allan and Rosie had to move away to receive other guests, Nicola said to Alex, 'Everyone knows you, don't they?'

He looked around him, smiling at the guests as he did so.

'Not everyone. . .but the patients. . .' He paused for a second. 'Allan and I have one or two friends who are not joint. Not a good idea to live in each other's pockets outside the practice. Ah, Sue. . . Harry. . .' A couple joined them, and he made the necessary introductions.

Nicola could not help noticing the look of faint surprise that flickered over their respective faces as they greeted her, in truth glad to see Alex *with* someone after his disastrous engagement.

Harry and Sue Courteney were good friends of Alex's, although they did not see a great deal of him. Harry was a radiologist and a delightful outgoing man of thirty-five, clever, good-humoured and well-liked. Sue, the same age, was a natural blonde with a very fair skin and deep blue eyes that lit up her small oval face. She studied Nicola with interest, liking what she saw but aware of a certain distant expression that set her apart from the rest of the gathering.

Alex felt that he owed it to their mutual friendship to put them in the picture a little about Nicola, particularly as he had not mentioned her previously and, without her realising it, Sue's gaze was enquiring.

'Nurse Hardy is by way of being my practice nurse, and a patient, so she is very much part of the scene here this evening. . .'

Sue Courteney looked genuinely interested and gave Nicola a warm smile, as though welcoming her to the circle.

Harry exclaimed with a little laugh, 'So you know the other side of the practice!'

'Very well,' Nicola assured him. 'It's very different from hospital life.'

Sue exclaimed, 'So you were a hospital nurse! I do admire you. . . Alex, we've hardly seen you lately. . . I know!' she laughed. 'The doctor's perfect alibi—the word "busy". . . How about rectifying the possibility of further delays by coming over to lunch one Sunday?' She looked directly at Alex, having noticed that he and Nurse Hardy had arrived together, 'And you too, Nurse Hardy. Any friend of Alex is a friend of ours.'

Harry sounded enthusiastic as he made a murmur of assent.

Nicola liked them and accepted. It would be interesting to hear about Alex from his friends.

'How about Sunday week?' Sue asked persistently. She looked from face to face.

Alex took a slim diary from his pocket, glanced at it and then at Nicola. 'I'm all right. . .and you?'

'I know I'm free then,' she said, sipping her sherry and realising how empty her diary had been since Stuart went—due in the main to her own fault—while wondering, even so, if she really wanted to accept this invitation after all. These people were strangers to her. But the date was made and she could not do anything about it. They talked for a little longer and then agreed that they must circulate.

Nicola noticed the way several of Alex's patients gravitated towards him, the women eager for his attention, his profession like a magnet. He treated them with equal charm while remaining wisely aloof from their blandishments. Nicola found it amusing. She had never joined in the nurses' crushes on the doctors and consultants during her hospital days and was certainly not going to start now.

A voice at her elbow said with a faint chuckle, 'They all crowd around Dr Alex.' The dark-haired girl of about twenty looked at Nicola meaningly.

'He's a very good doctor,' Nicola said pleasantly.

'I don't think it's his medical qualifications they're paying homage to... I'm Felicity Vaughan. I'm a medical secretary at Cheltenham General.'

Nicola introduced herself and added, 'I'm Dr Alex's practice nurse.'

The round blue eyes twinkled, the neat eyebrows raised.

'You're to be envied.'

Nicola felt a little irritated.

'Dr Alex is a very kind man,' she said a little stiffly.

Felicity Vaughan didn't mince matters, 'That is rather like calling pink champagne "pleasant"!'

A man's voice demanded, 'And what is that intriguing statement supposed to mean?'

'This is my fiancé, Gerald Fortesque,' came the smooth announcement.

Nicola liked him. He had an easy-to-read face, with frank green eyes and the expression of a man who laughed without effort. A man, she thought instinctively, one would trust—and then, cynically, scorned her own naïveté. 'Trust' was a demoted word in her own vocabulary.

'I still want to know *what* is like calling pink champagne "pleasant",' he insisted after he and Nicola had exchanged greetings.

Felicity told him and gave a meaning chuckle.

'Even as a mere man, I see what you mean,' he agreed.

Alex moved across the room and joined the little circle. He was friendly with the couple and they talked naturally. Nicola found that she was listening more than joining in the conversation, conscious of Allan and Rosie as they moved easily among their guests, until a few minutes later Allan took up a position in the centre of the room, Rosie beside him, as the gathering hushed and all eyes turned upon the two figures standing there.

Allan said, his voice ringing with pride, 'I want you all to know that Rosie is going to marry me and we thought this was a good way of announcing our engagement.'

Nicola heard the words and her heart seemed to miss a beat. Her gaze was instinctively drawn to Alex and it held as though they were sympathising with each other. Yet in his expression there was no pain, but rather a look of concern for her which, while she appreciated it, she did not want to accept. In that second she remembered her own engagement party which her parents had given. She wondered if Alex had celebrated in the same fashion, but with his father doing the honours. She had not heard any mention of his broken engagement that evening and his manner made it easy to forget the fact. She stood there, bleak and uncertain, while putting on a bright smile as she added her good wishes to all the others.

Allan and Rosie exchanged a faintly apprehensive glance. In their own happiness they had overlooked Alex's and Nicola's position.

'This,' said Alex as he found himself at Nicola's side after having spoken to the happy couple, 'is one engagement that won't be broken.'

Nicola's emotions were churned up and emphasised disillusionment; she wanted to lash out in order to bandage her own wounds.

'You have more faith in human nature than I,' she retorted. 'I'm surprised.'

Alex criticised himself for having made the observation, and did not miss the overt reference to himself.

'It's a bad thing to allow hurt to feed on disillusionment.'

Her eyes flashed as she exclaimed, 'Hurt stabs at different depths!'

She expected a challenge, but he said quietly, 'There are many depths of love. That's where the test comes in.' His gaze met hers and held it. 'You think I've overlooked that?'

It was the last thing she expected him to say.

'I find it difficult to assess your feelings,' she countered. Her voice had a slightly critical tone.

'At some level and in some circumstances we are all strangers to each other,' he suggested. But he knew, even as he spoke, that his ideal relationship was one of close communication at every level and he did not dwell on the fact that he and Karen had not achieved it, despite his love for her. In retrospect these facts revealed themselves.

Betty and Julie appeared beside them, having watched the changing expressions on their respective faces and feeling the irony of the situation.

Alex smiled at them. 'Well? Did you expect this announcement?'

Slight embarrassment touched them. They had; but they couldn't forget that he and Nicola had both been rejected and that this must be an ironical moment.

'It had occurred to us,' Betty said honestly. 'Just

something about Dr Forbes——' She broke off awkwardly.

Julie said in her forthright manner, 'You cannot hide happiness. It puts a stamp on you.' She gave a little half-hearted laugh. 'I'm minus stamps, but I live in hope.' She looked slightly sheepish after she had made the remark.

No one spoke and the two of them moved away.

Alex, aware of the stillness in Nicola's manner and feeling a certain depression on his own account, said, 'Would you like to cut out dinner and go home?'

Womanlike, Nicola became alert. Had his generosity in inviting her in the first place worn thin, and was he tired of her company?

'Not unless you are bored at the prospect of——'

'That,' he immediately protested, 'doesn't come into it.'

The words rushed out before she could prevent them. 'You thought it would do me good to get out and——'

He cut in. 'I did not go out of my way,' he reminded her sharply, 'to accompany you here.'

She flushed and knew she deserved the rebuke. Her voice was subdued as she admitted, 'I would like to keep to the arrangement.' She felt mollified and was at a loss to know why she so resented the possibility of his doing her a favour.

Rosie detached herself from a little group and came to their side, looking anxiously from face to face, knowing it was a delicate situation which, in her own excitement and happiness, she had overlooked earlier.

'A few friends will stay on,' she said with enthusiasm, 'we'd love you to——'

Alex cut in swiftly, 'We're going to have a meal at the Queen's, thank you all the same.'

That made Rosie feel better. Nicola noticed the sapphire and diamond ring on Rosie's left hand—it had appeared miraculously after the announcement, having been kept in a discreet hiding-place meanwhile. Nicola thought that it was the little things that hurt, as she looked down at her own bare finger.

'We must arrange something,' Rosie said easily, aware of the fact that Alex had been strictly alone during the past months.

Alex noticed that Nicola didn't comment on the idea. He was left to smile and nod.

Allan joined them, buoyant, beaming, telling himself that neither Alex nor Nicola would be single for very long, and glad that at least they had come to the party together. There was, however, nothing in their respective demeanours to even hint at more than friendship. They exchanged pleasantries for a few seconds, then parted, Alex and Nicola putting their glasses down with finality as they said goodbye, nodding across the room to Harry and Sue, Betty and Julie, Gerald Fortesque and Felicity Vaughan, before making a somewhat relieved exit.

'One needs an extra pair of feet for these occasions,' Nicola said a little later as they settled in the car for the short run to the hotel, her mood changing, as she was aware of Alex's silence and solemn expression.

The Queen's Hotel stood imposingly at the head of the Promenade, a gleaming illuminated white colonnaded building, overlooking the magnificent Imperial Gardens with its masses of flowerbeds carved squarely amid lush green lawns, and beautified by massive trees which stood sentinel over the scene. It had been named in honour of Queen Victoria and opened in 1838.

Nicola tensed. She had deliberately shut her thoughts against the fact that she and Stuart had visited it on several occasions, but it was more part of the general scene where her parents and their mutual friends had used it. She wondered if Alex had any similar memories. He was completely relaxed as they entered the reception area from which could be seen the spectacular central staircase. She realised that he was well known there as the *maître d'hôtel* greeted him with a spontaneous welcome which embraced Nicola and gave the impression that they were the only guests.

They went into the Regency Restaurant, being given a table by one of the large oval windows which overlooked the Imperial Gardens. The glow from glittering chandeliers and wall lights shadowed the cream décor and floral arrangements, while small candelabra decorated the tables and shone on pink and white napery.

Waiters appeared with a menu and wine list.

Alex looked at Nicola.

'I think we'll stick to champagne tonight,' he said easily, handing back the wine list to the smiling waiter. 'Krug,' he nodded pleasantly.

There was something a little deliberate in his manner as he turned back to Nicola, as though he was willing her to enjoy the occasion.

They chose Lobster thermidor and a Grand Marnier soufflé. The ice bucket was brought and the champagne poured out. They raised their glasses. 'To Allan and Rosie,' he suggested.

Nicola's thoughts were in turmoil; she could not sustain one mood for more than a few minutes and resented the hurt that lay just beneath the surface of her smile. She knew she had been ungracious, a characteristic that was normally foreign to her, and she said impulsively, 'May I ask my doctor a question?'

He was instantly alert; his gaze serious.

'Do.'

'Is there a tonic for being out of tune with life?' She tried to sound professional.

'Nothing that comes in a bottle,' he said immediately. 'Being banal, I'd say that laughter was the finest tonic, even when you feel you haven't anything to laugh about.'

She sipped her champagne and, looking at him with an appealing gaze, asked, 'Do you take your own medicine?'

There was a tense silence before he replied, 'I try to. You have to make friends with the "slings and arrows",' he quoted, 'before you can make any real progress.'

She dared to persist, 'And do you feel you have already *made* progress?'

At that moment a beautiful, striking girl of about twenty-five, followed by an older, well-groomed, pleased-with-himself man, walked towards their table on their way out.

Nicola saw Alex start and knew it was his ex-fiancée.

CHAPTER FOUR

ALEX was not prepared for the shock of seeing Karen, and for a second their gazes met, startled, and fell away as she passed the table without any acknowledgement. It struck him even in that split second that she was a very attractive girl, but he was not stirred by the fact so much as by the memories of the first shattering disillusionment when she had broken their engagement and left him devastated. He waited for his heart to quicken its beat, for a sensation of loss to overwhelm him, but the emotion didn't come. Instead a strange unreality crept upon him, as though the experience had happened in another life, and he was standing back looking upon a scene from which he was divorced. He was aware of Nicola's gaze upon him and that he must offer an explanation for his sudden transfixed state.

'That,' he said smoothly, 'was my ex-fiancée. I've no doubt you guessed.'

Nicola thought of how she would feel had Stuart walked past with Sarah Robertson, and shuddered at the prospect.

She didn't hesitate as she said, 'Yes. . . I'm sorry.'

'Don't be; we were bound to see each other at some time. It is rather a revealing experience.' His voice was steady, his expression confident.

Nicola felt slightly irritated by his attitude which in no way conformed to her idea of a natural reaction and left her with the idea that his feelings were, after all, shallow, and that his sympathy for her had in no way reflected a mutual suffering, but rather a kindness stemming from a general understanding.

And as they spoke Alex was asking himself if love could leave one so untouched, and was even prepared to accept that he'd had a lucky escape. When it came to it, he argued, Karen had none of the virtues which he had first attributed to her. She was a mercenary who grasped at material assets, counting love as nought. He faced the fact that he had been infatuated, shocked and, now, relieved. If he had nurtured any lingering passion, this incident had cured him. His heartbeat was regular and his mind cleared of doubt. It had been an unpleasant experience to which 'finis' had been written.

He found Nicola's steady, somewhat critical gaze unnerving. It cancelled his instinctive intention of confiding his feelings, so that he fell back on inscrutability.

'Human nature is very unpredictable; one's reactions are seldom as one imagines them being.'

'And you,' she countered somewhat tartly, 'are not easy to assess.'

He smiled inwardly. How like a woman to be annoyed because her sympathy was not needed! How obvious it was that she would have appreciated being able to understand and share what she imagined would be his distress; and how obvious, also, that she would have been bereft had she seen Stuart in similar circumstances. The possibility irritated him without his realising it.

'We are,' he said with a somewhat challenging air, 'mysteries to each other when it comes to emotion.' He raised his eyebrows and smiled as he added, 'To say nothing of ourselves.'

He noticed the shadow that crossed her face and the resistant expression that came into her eyes, his interest sharpening on her attitude. He realised that she wanted the solace of sharing an experience with him at the same level, so their relationship would be neatly tabulated and devoid of any sexual overtones. He told himself he was quite content to leave it at that. His desire to console her was absolutely genuine.

'I don't agree with you,' she said bluntly.

He made a little gesture and sipped his champagne. 'Your privilege,' he said smoothly and in no mood to argue, which he knew Nicola would have liked.

It wasn't the reaction she either expected or desired and she looked at him stormily, her earlier mood returning, cutting out any harmony. She didn't know what she expected of this man, but if he said black her instinct was to say white, and it infuriated her because she sensed that he knew it and had no intention of pandering to what he would call her moods. It seemed important that what she had considered to be the bond of their identical experience should be maintained.

'I envy you your ability to escape from the past unscathed.'

'It isn't a virtue to pander to suffering,' he retorted. He was aware of the light of battle in her eyes and was ready to meet it. She looked particularly attractive when she was angry and it gave him satisfaction to accept the challenge.

Nicola flushed, remembering his earlier solicitude and how good he had been to her. Now he sat there, confident and ready to criticise, and she knew they could easily be on the edge of a quarrel, finding that the possibility did not displease her.

'*Pandering* doesn't come into it,' she scoffed. 'It is a question of how deep one's feelings are. . . I'm glad you've obviously escaped so lightly.'

Alex resented that.

'If it suits you to think so. . .' He drew her gaze to his and studied her with an unnerving intensity, recognising that he found her stimulating as well as attractive and that her presence removed the shades of grey from his life. He hurried over the fact that his objective had been to help her and that he had been touched by her suffering, by implication suggesting that he, in his similar position, shared the handicap. Now, however, having been brought face to face with his ex-fiancée, he could no longer claim that to be so. Nevertheless, he argued, this was no time to withdraw his sympathy from her or take up the challenge so that discord ensued.

And, in turn, Nicola reflected that she had been particularly ungracious that evening and had misjudged him in the beginning when she thought in terms of his doing her a favour by inviting her out. Nevertheless, she did not want to make any move that would increase the familiarity.

She changed the subject.

'I don't know why your friends should have included me in their invitation to lunch,' she said abruptly.

Alex realised in that second that he was more than pleased it had been so.

'Harry and Sue?' he said warmly. 'You'll like them.'

He added deliberately, 'My ex-fiancée didn't appreciate them. They were not her type.'

'And you think they are mine?'

Alex asked himself if that were so and knew the answer was in the affirmative. There was a naturalness about Sue which he considered matched Nicola's easy manner. He also realised that he found it pleasurable to have Nicola associated with him.

'I think,' he said, holding her gaze, 'that you will have a lot in common. Sue paints—very well, as a matter of fact.'

Nicola stared at him.

'I don't paint,' she pointed out.

'But,' he said instinctively, 'you're artistic. I associate you with the artistic side of life rather than the material.' It occurred to him as he spoke that the assessment had been made wholly without thought, but he considered it valid.

'Being associated with medicine puts one in neither camp,' she suggested.

'But allows for being associated with either.' It seemed important to make the point. He knew that she wanted to be contrary.

And Nicola knew that she didn't want to be involved with his friends, or, for that matter, with anyone new, no matter from where they might originate. She shrank from the idea that he might be looking at the matter of Harry and Sue Courtney as representing a couple whose company and circle of friends might be 'good' for her, in the same way as he had told Jan that tonight's outing would be good for her. If it were not in the nature of a favour, then it was a method whereby she would be drawn into the world again and meet new people, and where he could continue his solicitude. She wondered how she could get out of going without being ungracious.

As though reading her thoughts he said deliberately, 'I shall look forward to it.' He hastened on irrelevantly, 'Reverting to the question of Harry and Sue.'

She made no comment, but felt his gaze intently upon her and averted her own somewhat uncomfortably.

Alex was telling himself that he would not tolerate any excuses should she attempt to avoid the lunch and was surprised by his own tenacity of purpose.

Nicola brought the conversation around to medicine.

'Why,' Alex asked, 'didn't you qualify?' He was suddenly anxious to know more of Nicola's professional and emotional background.

'Possibly lack of ambition; a too comfortable lifestyle for intensive study.' She paused.

'And?' he prompted, his dark eyes challenging her.

'The desire to marry and live happily ever after, like my parents.'

Alex found those words poignant; they emphasised the emptiness of her present position and the disillusionment that had led up to it.

'The one doesn't cancel the other. There are many happily married women doctors.' He added, 'I cannot visualise you as fulfilled in a purely domestic setting.'

'Since there is not going to be any domestic setting, your point cannot be proved.' She added with clipped forcefulness, 'I shall not put myself in the position of being betrayed again.' She looked at him almost aggressively. 'But I'm sure I shall eventually come to your wedding.'

His reply was unexpected.

'I'm heartened to think that you will be in my life when that happens.'

Alex felt a strange sensation of unreality when he thought of his being married. Emotion stirred and he was able to contemplate the prospect with a sudden unexpected hopefulness. A moment of sensuality sent a shudder over his body and he knew that he could not tolerate a celibate life. His experience with Karen had not deadened desire and he did not pretend, as he looked at Nicola, that in different circumstances she would not stimulate him physically. At the moment they were too involved with her unhappiness to open up such possibilities. He conjectured that, when roused, she would be passionate, never accepting half-measures in anything, her fierce loyalty being the barometer of her general reactions.

She startled him by saying, her gaze direct and a little challenging, 'And what is your final summing-up? You've been dissecting me these last few seconds.'

He didn't lower his gaze, which was disconcerting.

'I don't deny that. I was also analysing myself,' he added unnervingly, 'and deciding that I was not cut out for a celibate life.'

The momentary silence was tense. Nicola started, but her heartbeats didn't quicken. She was conscious of faint irritation because the last thing she wanted to discuss was anything of a sexual nature. She liked the protection of Alex's sympathy and understanding, and put aside his earlier statements, preferring to bury her head in the sand and cling to the familiar trend, not wanting to extend the boundaries of their present relationship by a verbal intimacy. Her expression was cool and withdrawn as she ignored his confidence by saying swiftly, 'This soufflé is delicious.'

He looked at her long and hard, silently communicating his awareness of her resistance to expanding the conversation. There was a significant half-smile on his face as he agreed.

Nicola flushed. He made her feel gauche. Suddenly she wanted to go home, to be alone. The thought of Stuart hurt her. The intimacy of dinner *à deux* reminded her of other evenings when she had believed the stars were hers. She looked wan, as though all vitality had been drained from her—a fact which Alex was quick to notice.

He said sympathetically, 'Despite the virtues of the soufflé, you are weary. I'm sorry,' he added, 'my conversation has not been altogether tactful. I've talked about myself—an error I try to avoid.'

'And mostly succeed in doing. . .' Her voice trailed away.

He accepted that.

'I'm afraid I'm horribly transparent at the moment,' she admitted, looking at him with an honest gaze. 'You have made it very easy for me to be.'

Their respective moods changed. In that instant she saw Dr Alex, her employer as well as a friend, while he saw the practice nurse on whom he had come to rely and for whom he had a sympathy. But that evening his feelings had been tempered with the steel of his own escape from heartache. Illusion had died with what had once appeared to be love. In a strange indescribable way he had become a free man again. Not one living in the shadow of a broken engagement—the object of sympathetic gossip. He realised that he was suddenly impatient for Nicola to escape from suffering and go out once again to meet life and happiness. This ambition had thrived from the moment he knew about Stuart, but it had gathered momentum since seeing Karen that evening, and the truth had shocked him with its brutal revelation.

'I shall have to take a sterner line,' he said masterfully.

She was instantly on the defensive.

'I do not take kindly to being manipulated.' Her voice was warning.

'Not even if it is to take you out of that cocoon of unhappiness?'

She protested, 'I'm not wrapping myself in any cocoon.'

'Aren't you, Nicola?' The way he uttered her name heightened the significance of his words. The insinuation annoyed her.

'No,' she protested, adding hotly, 'Just because you appear to have escaped unscathed is no reason why you should expect me to follow your example and be superior in the bargain.'

Alex liked her when she was annoyed and his pulse quickened as he retorted, 'I can't pretend for the sake of appearance, *or* to live up to your idea of what I *should* feel.'

'Could we change the subject?' she suggested tartly.

'By all means. At least you've come to life again.' His scrutiny unnerved her.

They reached the coffee stage, falling back on general conversation, practice problems, until it was time to leave.

In the silence of the taxi, Alex was aware of the delicately scented warmth of her body next to his, and his senses stirred. He didn't pretend to himself that she didn't attract him, while accepting the fact that it was normal and not indicative of anything serious.

'Thank you for this evening,' she said quietly as they reached home.

'The medicine was not too bad,' he suggested lightly.

'On the contrary, I liked the flavour. Champagne affects my moods and I hope I wasn't too frank.' She met his gaze in the illuminated darkness as he saw her out of the car.

His hand tightened on her elbow and she was conscious of his touch without response.

'You made yourself abundantly clear,' he replied with a half-smile as he saw her to the front door, opened it with her key and stood aside as she crossed the threshold. 'Goodnight, Nicola.'

She watched him go down the steps and back to the waiting car. She felt a sense of relief that the evening was over. The thought of Stuart stabbed.

'I hate hot weather,' came the outburst from Nicola's first, and new, patient the following Monday. A Mrs Sandra Foster, thirty-five. She sat down wearily and was obviously suggestive of weight loss. Nicola judged that, well, she would have been a chocolate-box pretty woman. Her nervousness was noticeable. 'I'm so *tired* and I'm sick of palpitations!'

Nicola looked sympathetic. She observed the protrusion of the eyeballs.

'And I'd like to see Dr Alex... You're new,' she hurried on. 'I haven't been here for a while, but I——' She stopped jerkily. 'I eat a lot and lose weight.'

'Let me check over the usual things,' Nicola said encouragingly.

'I shall still want to see Dr Alex.' It was a warning. She made an excessive movement of her hands.

'We'll arrange that,' Nicola promised soothingly, checking a rapid pulse.

'Now,' Mrs Foster insisted. 'I know his father, Philip Moncton.' The words came out in a rush.

'One moment,' Nicola said and, lifting the telephone receiver, spoke to Julie. Alex was between patients and Nicola got through to him.

'I can fit Mrs Foster in now,' he said helpfully.

When told, Mrs Foster looked pleased and self-satisfied. 'My husband hasn't any patience with me,' she said irrelevantly. 'Perhaps when I've seen Dr Alex he'll take me seriously. He says my eyes have always bulged; but they haven't. Blind creatures, men.'

Alex saw Nicola at lunchtime that day. The memory of the previous Saturday evening lay between them for a second before he said, 'Well; what did you think of Mrs Foster?'

'Thyrotoxicosis,' she said firmly. 'Graves's Disease.' She met his gaze.

'Correct,' he said, pleased. 'We'll do the tests and

then put her on to carbimazole—fifteen mg three times a day for three weeks.'

'Reducing to five mg three times a day, according to response, for at least twelve to eighteen months.'

He gave her an approving nod.

'A cousin of mind had it,' Nicola explained, 'and, of course, one comes up against it in hospital.'

He studied her a little unnervingly.

'All the same, you would have made a good doctor.'

They both remembered the reasons she had given for not qualifying.

A smile touched her lips.

'I'm doing the next best thing,' she reminded him. 'Helping in a practice.'

'Yes, thank heaven,' he said heartily. He didn't want to dwell on the prospect of her leaving and going in search of a new adventure, since there had been the suggestion that her job there had been of a temporary nature to help them out. She had become part of the team and he suddenly wanted to establish the fact.

'Does that satisfy you?' He hung on her reply.

She was immediately alerted, not wishing to commit herself.

'For the present,' she replied guardedly.

He held her gaze, accepting the fact that he wanted a commitment.

'You once implied that you might consider a permanency.'

There was a moment of silence which she broke by saying, 'We were talking generally.'

He reflected as he stood there that she was an elusive person and that her experience with Stuart had accentuated the quality. He, on the other hand, liked stability and a map for the future. Vague promises irritated him, a reaction stimulated by his own recent experience. The possibility of Nicola leaving sharpened his feelings almost to a point of dismay, which astounded him; but then, he argued, he always had hated staff changes. He liked a close-knit unit about which he didn't have to worry.

'Just so long as you give us time to replace you,' he said a trifle stiffly to conceal his apprehension.

'I promise I'll keep you in the picture and should never leave you in the lurch.' She continued, 'Unless it was something beyond my control.'

He nodded his appreciation, and a feeling of relief touched him. He told himself that, unless the practice was secure and running smoothly, peace of mind was impossible. It didn't occur to him that he had never before given the practice nurse such importance, even while accepting her as a very necessary member of the staff.

'I hope the future will be free from all complications,' he suggested.

She looked at him with renewed interest. Events of the previous evening had established him in a new light, emphasising his compassion for her and the fact that she had imagined his being far more deeply involved with his ex-fiancée than was actually the case, judging him by his attitude. She didn't want to dwell on the fact because it alienated the former bond of their mutual suffering and gave him a separate identity, which precluded her from regarding him as a fellow sufferer, divorced from any possibility of the man-woman relationship which she shunned.

Jan said on the evening of the following day, 'I met Alex this morning as I was coming out of Cavendish House.' This was *the* store in the Promenade, with its wide front, clock and hanging baskets.

Nicola looked up from the magazine she was reading. Jan thought she was instantly alert.

'I don't associate Alex with shopping,' she said without smiling.

'He said he'd been buying shirts.' There was a faint pause before Jan added, 'I invited him to supper this Thursday.' She hastened, 'I should have made it lunch on Sunday, but I know you're going to the Courtneys'.' Jan wanted it to sound wholly natural.

Nicola asked bluntly, 'Did he accept?'

'Why, yes.'

'I don't want the Sunday do.'

Jan was guarded.

'Any particular reasons? I've heard of the Courtneys; they're supposed to be a very delightful couple.'

'I'm sure they are, but just because I happened to be with Alex was no reason why they should have included me.' It was an almost belligerent sound. She added, 'What made you ask Alex to supper?'

Jan remained cool.

'Because Timothy and I like him and it's been mentioned in a general sort of way.'

Nicola felt awkward.

'I might be going out with Julie.'

Jan didn't make any protest. She knew Nicola's mood.

'Your father and I are quite capable of entertaining Alex,' she countered. 'You didn't come into it.' Nevertheless both Jan and Timothy had it in mind to create opportunities whereby Alex and Nicola might be together outside the practice. Alex was a man they liked and appreciated doubly after the defects of Stuart.

Nicola made no comment and then, after a minute, said surprisingly, 'I might bring Julie home and join you.' It was a statement uttered half as a question.

'By all means.' Jan was imperturbable.

'She thinks Alex is terribly attractive.'

'Which is not surprising, since that seems to be the consensus of opinion.' Jan looked at Nicola directly. 'Don't you agree?'

Nicola made a little scoffing sound.

'I'm in no mood to see any man as attractive,' she said bitterly.

Jan didn't hesitate. 'Stuart isn't worth that bitterness. You're still giving him far too much importance, Nicola.'

Nicola's voice rose.

'I loved him and can't suddenly pretend he didn't exist.' She added hotly, 'Not like some people.'

Jan looked enquiring. 'Meaning?'

Nicola told Jan of the episode with Alex and Karen, not having intended doing so, finishing with, 'So I don't think we need waste our sympathy on Alex. He's not nursing a broken heart.' It was said almost aggressively. In truth, when summing up she, Nicola, felt she had lost an ally without losing his sympathy and moral support.

'I'm glad to hear it,' Jan said immediately. She added deliberately, 'The right woman will come along and she'll be very lucky.'

Nicola lowered her gaze. Alex's kindness to her supported the belief, but she had no intention of seeing him other than as a supportive friend with whom she would never get involved. She recalled his words about not being cut out for a celibate life, denigrating the possibility of her ever feeling sexually attracted to any man again.

Julie said, when Nicola invited her for supper on Thursday, 'I'd have loved to come, but I've just met a dishy man who is taking me out to a meal. Something in computers. He was at the club I've joined.' She laughed. 'The one you wouldn't go to. Name Barry Jones. Very respectable. Twenty-eight.'

'Oh, good,' Nicola said brightly, adding with a laugh, 'Not that you can't come to supper, but that you've made a friend.'

Julie's eyes twinkled and she grinned.

'You could say that. . .thank your mother for the invitation.'

'Very formal,' Nicola chipped in. 'You must bring Barry Jones along some time.' Nicola felt a pang. She would miss the idea of Julie being free.

'I'd like to.' Julie looked pleased. 'Barry wants me to meet his parents.'

Nicola could not help saying, 'That gives it the seal of respectability and will tell you a little about him.' She was defensive in Julie's cause.

Julie knew she was being warned.

'Don't worry.' She met Nicola's gaze fearlessly, 'I know all the pitfalls. Experience is a good teacher.'

Nicola gave a disparaging grunt.

'Is that why people invariably repeat their mistakes? The only safe way is to——'

Julie interrupted a little sharply, 'You can't cut sex out of your life and live like a nun.' She added, 'There's got to be trust somewhere.'

'You're an optimist.' The words came cynically.

Julie simply said, 'Yes.' She felt it would end the conversation, and it did.

Nicola envied Julie her confident air as she watched her swing out of the common-room. A horrible empty feeling made her depressed.

Alex startled her as he appeared in the doorway, having bumped into Julie.

'A pleasant, cheerful receptionist,' he observed with a smile. 'We all make a good team.'

Nicola agreed.

'I'm going to have supper with you this Thursday.' Alex spoke with pleasurable anticipation.

'With Timothy and Jan,' she said pointedly.

He held her gaze.

'Meaning that you won't be there?' It was in the nature of a challenge.

'As far as I know I shall be there.' It was a tentative reply.

He accepted that and said deliberately, 'I like your parents enormously, as I've said before. Their company is always stimulating and a pleasure.'

She smiled her agreement, while feeling she had

made the point that her being there on Thursday was purely incidental. It struck her that she would be with him both on Thursday and at the Courtneys' on the Sunday, but experienced no thrill at the prospect.

Alex accepted her attitude and their brief conversation ended with his saying suddenly and irrelevantly, 'Mrs Gordon was pregnant. You were right. There's great rejoicing because they've been trying for over a year.'

Nicola stiffened. She and Stuart had talked of having at least two children.

Alex saw the shadow that crossed her face and was surprised to feel a slight impatience because it was obvious to him that she was thinking of Stuart and what might have been. No situation or set of circumstances contributed to a change of heart, or lightening of her spirits.

'I'm glad for them,' she commented flatly.

He looked at her as she stood there, attractive in her uniform—a challenge and a temptation. She was not the type a man could ignore, he thought, or comfortably dismiss, and it irritated him to have to accept the fact. He gave her a hard look, muttered something about work and went back to his consulting-room, where he sat down at his desk, flicked his paperknife up and down on the large blotting pad, at a loss to understand his reactions. Then, telling himself that he'd allowed Nicola to play on his sympathies for too long, he sent for the next patient. At least, he argued aggressively, one knew where one was with patients, no matter how difficult they might sometimes be.

Nicola thought, as Alex came into the flat that

Thursday, that he always seemed perfectly at home there, and brought with him an air of gaiety, rather like a schoolboy let out of school. But on this occasion he said seriously, 'I'm afraid I've had to have the calls transferred here—do you mind?'

Timothy reassured him.

'My father has an important committee meeting and Allan and Rosie have seats for the theatre.' He added, 'With luck it may be quiet.' He had already made himself comfortable in one of the deep armchairs and restricted himself to a small sherry.

Nicola studied him. She supposed he *was* an attractive man, even as Jan had insisted. But, she told herself, he could have three heads and it would not make any difference to her own reactions. Her emotions had been bruised, and that deadened any sexual awareness. She sat there detached, listening more than talking as her parents enjoyed their conversation over supper.

'You're very quiet,' Alex said, looking at her somewhat anxiously.

'I'm in a listening mood,' she countered with a slow smile, suddenly restless under his intense scrutiny. His dark eyes met hers and their gaze held for a second, awakening a nervousness she was at a loss to understand.

The telephone rang. They had finished their meal.

'I thought it was too good to last!' Alex exclaimed as Timothy got up from the table to answer it and within seconds, for the telephone was at hand, said, 'One moment.' Turning to Alex, he nodded and Alex got to his feet to take the receiver.

A distraught girl whom he knew cried, 'I'm miscarrying...and alone. Oh, Dr Alex, please come!'

'I'll be with you in a few minutes.' He was careful not to mention a name and replaced the receiver, turning regretfully as he said, 'I'm awfully sorry. Afraid it's urgent.'

Nicola got to her feet.

'Can I be of any help?'

He looked at her, his manner grateful.

'Yes,' he said, 'I'd be thankful to have you.' There was a note of relief in his deep voice.

CHAPTER FIVE

ALEX and Nicola arrived at Charlotte Grantham's flat, near the attractive tree-lined Tivoli Road, in record time. He said en route, 'I've had very little to do with Miss Grantham, so don't know any of the circumstances. I treat her parents, who are of the old school.' He stopped the car and glanced at the solid converted Victorian house, which stood back from the pavement and grass verge. He grabbed his bag, and he and Nicola hurried to the communal entrance where a large heavy front door stood open.

Nicola looked at the information panel, saying, 'Charlotte Grantham, second floor, flat three.'

Alex's gaze met hers; it told her that he was glad she was with him.

The front door was unlocked and they went in as arranged. The patient, twenty-three, hollow-eyed, pale and distressed, lay in a double bed in a light airy room with its colour scheme of peach and pink. Normally she was very attractive, with sparkling blue eyes and a vibrant personality. Now, all strength was drained from her and her voice was weak and apologetic. 'I'm so sorry to. . .trouble you, Dr Moncton, but I got frightened on my own,' she finished pathetically.

Alex's words came consolingly. 'No question of trouble. I'm your doctor and I've brought Nurse Hardy along to help you.' He took her pulse and blood-pressure; the former rapid, the latter raised.

'When did this start?' He made a cursory examination.

'About an hour ago. At first I thought it was a particularly heavy period. . . I have them very often and am irregular.' Fear mingled with the pain in her eyes. 'I was horrified when I realised what was happening.'

'We must get you to hospital immediately!' Alex exclaimed promptly.

She cried out, 'Oh, no! *No*. Please, Dr Moncton. . . My parents mustn't know; they'd be so appalled and condemnatory. I could stay here and——'

'Out of the question,' he said with a quiet firmness. 'As for your parents, leave them to me. I will explain the situation—visit them. The only thing that matters is seeing you have proper attention.' He studied her with solicitude, wondering where the man came into the picture—as did Nicola.

And although Charlotte Grantham looked grateful she rushed on, 'You see, they don't like Mark—the man I'm going to marry. We have been engaged for six months and neither he nor I knew I was—was pregnant. He's in London at the moment.' She went on disjointedly, 'He's in publishing, and is attending a book fair. . . My parents were dreadful when I took this flat and left home——' She broke off, adding wretchedly, 'Hospital. . . I'm stained and——'

Nicola told her quickly, 'I'll take care of all that, don't worry.'

A wave of faintness and increase of pain brought

forth a weak, 'Thank you.' Then, 'If I can't stay here, could you get me into the Cotswold Nursing Home? I know a sister there and——' Her voice broke and she realised she was incapable of looking after herself; and, even if she could stay in the flat, the prospect of her mother's being in charge horrified her. She could imagine the condemnatory, forbidding air.

Alex didn't hesitate. 'That would be simple,' he said immediately. 'We use the home quite a bit. I'll telephone them and arrange for an ambulance. While I'm doing that——'

Nicola said reassuringly, 'I'll get you ready, Miss Grantham.' She added, 'And I'll go with you and see you installed.'

'You're so kind,' came the appreciative words. 'It's my parents——' It was an agitated cry.

Alex said with gentle firmness, 'As I've told you, leave all that to me. Only you matter at the moment.' He left them, having ascertained that there was a telephone in the sitting-room.

Nicola slipped back into her nursing routine, washing, changing the stained nightdress, finding clean linen in the cupboards and making the patient comfortable.

Charlotte Grantham talked disjointedly. 'You see, I'd no idea I was pregnant. . . I wasn't sick or anything and I'm so irregular that two months. . . Oh, Nurse; you're so good to do all this. . . Mark's at a dinner tonight——' Her eyes were wide and anxious. 'He'll ring——' her eyes pleaded for guidance '—when he gets back to the Waldorf—that's where he's staying—and when he can't get me——'

'I'll contact the hotel and leave a message for him to

ring me,' Nicola suggested, 'then I can put him in the picture. You can speak to him yourself tomorrow.'

A hand reached out in gratitude. 'His name is Mark Benson, room forty-five.' The pain-racked eyes glistened. 'We love each other so *much*...can you understand?'

Nicola was grateful when Alex joined them at that moment, his knock preventing comment.

'Everything is arranged,' he said reassuringly, 'and the ambulance will be here in a few minutes.' He went on, 'I shall go immediately to see your parents, so that they will be in the picture.'

'Thank you...thank you.' The words rushed out brokenly. 'I'd not want them worried, whatever they may say.' She winced and lapsed into an exhausted silence. A short while later she was wrapped in blankets and put in the ambulance, Nicola pausing at the doors a second before joining her. Alex stood by, looking down into her eyes with faint anxiety and concern.

'You've got to get home.' His voice was low and almost alarmed.

'Plenty of taxis,' she assured him, aware of his attitude. She felt that he had it in mind to accompany them in order finally to see her home.

'I've put Father on call. He was fortunately back early,' he said as though it was relevant to his thoughts.

But Nicola stepped quickly into the ambulance. The doors shut and it raced away.

Alex stood very still for a moment until it was lost to sight. He thought how satisfying it had been to have Nicola working with him.

* * *

To Nicola's surprise Alex called to see her just after half-past nine that evening, apologising to Timothy and Jan for disturbing them. They understood, and he went into Nicola's sitting-room at their behest, aware of the look of amazement on Nicola's face as she saw him standing a little hesitantly in the doorway.

'I wanted to make sure you got home without any trouble. Taxis are, or can be, erratic, even at nursing homes.'

She stared at him a trifle critically.

'Aren't you rather forgetting that I'm used to going about in London? The idea that I need protecting in Cheltenham isn't without humour.'

He held her gaze, his expression disarming. 'Are you averse to being protected?'

'I'm averse to fuss,' she warned him.

'Point taken.' He hastened on, 'I wanted to know how you got on.'

Her eyebrows raised. 'No problems. The patient was grateful to be taken care of.' Nicola indicated a chair and they sat down.

'Can I offer you a drink?' She wondered why she had made the suggestion, not really wishing to prolong his visit, which she considered unnecessary in any case.

'A very small brandy would be welcome.'

She indicated the decanters on the drinks tray. 'I'll leave it to you.'

He walked towards the table. 'And you?'

'The same,' she murmured.

Glasses in hand, they settled down and he said suddenly, 'Are you still in a "listening mood"?'

She remembered her words earlier that evening.

'You have an excellent memory.' A look of surprise came into her eyes.

'For important things—yes,' he answered deliberately.

She flashed, 'I hardly call that important.' Why couldn't it be Stuart sitting there? Why this man? His solicitude irritated her, even though she criticised herself for the fact.

His words came deliberately, 'It is to me. I'd like your answer.'

'I think that depends on the subject matter.' Her voice was guarded.

'My talk to the Granthams.'

'Oh!' She didn't quite know why she was disappointed. 'How did they take it?'

He looked at her and shook his head. 'Badly and harshly. No wonder Miss Grantham dreaded their knowing.'

Nicola burst out, 'I marvel she bothers with them.'

He looked at her a trifle critically.

'Parents like that have a strange hold over their offspring. They instil guilt. An uncomfortable thing to live with.' He added significantly, 'You are in a singularly fortunate position with your parents.'

'I don't need reminding of that.' Her voice was firm and strong, her expression loving. A strange sensation surged over her. She and Stuart had never slept together. A little shiver went through her as she thought of him and Sarah Robertson being lovers. She felt Alex's gaze upon her as though he were reading her thoughts and she shrank from the intimacy that crept into the atmosphere, drawing them together despite her resistance.

'The Granthams are not going to the nursing home,' Alex explained.

Nicola gave a little cry of dismay. 'Oh, *no!*'

Alex recalled the bitterness with which the mother had made the announcement, adding that if her daughter chose to live 'in that immoral fashion', she must take the consequences and not expect any mercy. It had been like taking part in an old-fashioned melodrama and nothing Alex could say influenced her.

'Mr Grantham would have been more lenient, but his wife obviously dominates him. They both bear a grudge because Miss Grantham has a flat, and always knew no good would come of it,' Alex finished somewhat drily. 'If I hadn't been their doctor they would have behaved in an even more aggressive fashion. After a tirade against Mark Benson, they had the good grace to thank me for the trouble I'd taken in putting them in the picture. . . I've wondered about him.' He queried, 'Did you come to any arrangement as to how he was to be contacted?'

Nicola told him of the situation and that she had already left a message at the Waldorf.

He looked serious.

Nicola studied him.

'You take a great deal of interest in the lives of your patients,' she observed.

'You make that sound almost critical.' His voice dropped, but had a challenge in it. The atmosphere between them tensed. 'You cannot rule out emotion and deal with the purely physical.'

'Concentrating on the emotional can sometimes produce a nervous wreck,' she countered.

'I wasn't aware that I made nervous wrecks of my patients.' His expression was a little grim. He would have liked to remind her that *she* had needed understanding and sympathy recently.

Nicola felt mean and hastened, 'I expressed myself badly.' Their eyes met. 'You are a very compassionate doctor.'

The telephone rang. Nicola had her own line. She thought it would be too early for Mark Benson, but as she answered the call he gave his name, mystified by the request to call her. He had a strong, attractive voice which she liked. He explained that he had escaped from the dinner to telephone, having spoken to the hotel to see if there were any messages.

Nicola gave him the news reassuringly and sympathetically. His alarm and surprise came over forcefully. Having absorbed the shock, he said he would return at once. Nicola suggested that he speak to Alex, who took the receiver from her and outlined the procedure. Mark Benson said he would drive straight to the nursing home. Alex liked his manner and arranged a meeting with him in the morning. He felt that he was dealing with a reliable man whose anxiety was deep, and his gratitude for all that had been done sincere.

Nicola took the receiver a second or two later and ended the call. Her gaze was questioning as she returned to her chair and looked at Alex.

'Unless I'm very much mistaken, he will give his fiancée all the support she needs. I like his attitude.'

Nicola's voice held a trace of cynicism. 'Let's hope you're right. I don't profess to be a judge any more.'

'Just prejudiced,' Alex suggested, adding, 'in general.'

She didn't contradict him.

Alex was acutely aware of her as she sat there. Despite her friendliness there was a remoteness about her which proclaimed her untouchable. The fact irritated him, but a reluctance to leave immobilised him. He wanted to talk intimately, to break down the barrier created by her seeming sexlessness. He thought, inwardly furious, that she was a young, tremendously attractive girl and, as such, a challenge to his sexuality. As his gaze rested on her lips he knew that he wanted to take her in his arms and kiss her. Passion endangered his control.

The atmosphere changed as she became conscious of his nearness and the intensity of his expression.

'He's driving to the nursing home at once,' Alex said jerkily, breaking the tension, 'and seeing me tomorrow. No question of business coming first.'

Nicola felt a stab of jealousy. If only Stuart had been different. The old feeling of having been cheated surged back to darken her mood. She didn't want to look in the mirror and see love and happiness through other eyes, nor have to listen to Alex extolling it. Also, his gaze unnerved her, and she was resistant to it. Deliberately, she looked at the carriage clock on the table near by. He read her thoughts and said a trifle curtly, 'It's time for me to go.'

She made no attempt to stop him and he got to his feet. She followed and stood beside him. Eyes met eyes, and he was conscious of the fragrant warmth stealing from her body, and the desire that quickened his heartbeat.

'Thank you for coming,' she said coolly. 'I'm glad you were able to speak to Mr Benson. I shall visit Miss Grantham tomorrow.'

Emotion died in the face of the quiet efficiency of her voice.

Alex tried to sound impersonal. 'Thank you for your help tonight.'

'That is what nurses are for.' She didn't feel like giving an inch. 'Goodnight, Alex.'

He looked wholly inscrutable.

'Goodnight, Nicola. I can see myself out.' With that he strode away.

She stood there, feeling uneasy and inhospitable, but glad that he had gone. She didn't know why she always wanted to argue with him, or why he made the loss of Stuart so much more acute.

Nicola made a conscious effort to enjoy Sunday lunch with Harry and Sue Courtney. She liked them and they were good company, living in a charming house, half-timbered and of Cotswold stone, on the Winchcombe Road. An atmosphere of happiness hung delightfully over it and their harmony was obvious. A pang shot through Nicola as she looked at them together and she felt instinctively that they were deliberately making her doubly welcome because she was with Alex. She envied him his relaxed air, while finding that, for all the hospitality, she was tense and on edge as they tentatively suggested a visit to the Everyman Theatre and mentioned various restaurants to which they might go in future. Alex received their ideas with enthusiasm, while Nicola hoped that a smile would suffice. She talked as much as was polite, thanked them warmly for their welcome and left gratefully, as though she had come through an ordeal.

Alex said on the way back, 'You were very subdued.' There was a note of criticism in his voice. 'Didn't you enjoy yourself?'

She couldn't be blunt and reply that she was there with the wrong man, but just flashed him a glance and said frankly, 'I'm not in the mood for social gatherings.'

'Or those *á deux*,' he retorted. He didn't take his eyes off the road as he added, 'It's the beginning of September.' The statement was significant.

Faint colour crept into her cheeks.

'Meaning that memory is not allowed to live after a few months.'

'No,' he said firmly, 'but that if you withdraw from life and people——'

She cut in hotly, 'Just because I don't enthuse about everyone, or want a series of wild parties——' She broke off impatiently, annoyed because she allowed him to irritate her, which she knew was all wrong in view of his kindness and consideration.

His laughter was low and a trifle teasing. 'I can't see you at a wild party——'

'Don't be patronising,' she snapped.

He stiffened. Since the night of the miscarriage, he had been conscious of her to a disturbing degree, unable to maintain a casual pleasant atmosphere, and wanting to rise to every occasion when she attacked.

'Coming out with me doesn't improve your temper,' he challenged.

She knew that was true and was ashamed because she allowed it to be so obvious; ashamed, also, that she could not stop wishing that Stuart was beside her, knowing it to be foolish and weak. She shrank from any evidence of Alex's interest in her beyond that of the purely platonic. And she had sensed, that evening at the flat, that emotion had momentarily manifested itself. There had been no recurrence. They had maintained an almost professional attitude until now.

'I'm not very good company,' she admitted honestly, adding in a conciliatory tone, 'I'll make up for it next time.'

Alex found the words 'next time' encouraging.

'Allan and Rosie want us to join them for an evening next week,' he told her. 'I promised I'd discuss it with you,' he finished hopefully.

There was a moment's silence before she said, trying to overcome an instinctive reluctance, 'That would be enjoyable. I can fit in with whatever plans they care to make.'

It seemed easier to be with people with whom she was familiar than to break new ground with strangers.

'Oh, fine!' Alex sounded please. 'I'm glad you and Rosie are such good friends.'

'It would be very difficult not to like Rosie,' Nicola said warmly. 'She and Allan are well suited.' She hastened as though having made a concession, 'We shall see.'

Alex observed drily, 'You can't bear to give an inch, can you?'

'Wisdom is tempered with reservation.'

'Then you must be very wise,' he said with feeling.

Nicola gave him a sideways glance, aware that there was a half-smile on his face and that his profile was chiselled and attractive.

'I,' she scoffed, 'have never been wise, or I shouldn't be where I am now.'

'A compliment indeed!' he retorted, his voice sharp.

She hastened, 'I didn't mean it like that. . . I expressed myself badly. I was just reflecting on my life and poor judgement of character in the past. Working for you. . .' She paused.

He put in, emotion rising, 'Is the bread and butter of your life.' He waited, tensed, for her comment.

She rose to that immediately, without thinking of any denigration.

'Exactly right. One has a solid foundation in bread and butter, and no pretence.'

He knew she was divorced from passion, or any sexual stimulation, and saw in the simile a perfect example of what she wanted from life at that moment.

'And dullness,' he suggested on a note of disgust, irritation besetting him.

She flashed him a faintly disdainful look.

'Dullness can be a panacea after a thunderstorm of emotion.' She spoke sharply, almost warningly.

Alex pressed his foot harder on the accelerator.

'It can also be deadly.'

'Meaning,' she flashed, 'that I'm boring.'

He didn't pretend.

'Your outlook is,' he said without hesitation, adding, 'There'll come a moment when you want to scream at the memory of all this.' His pause was significant. 'Then it will be too late.'

Nicola was to remember his words. . .

Both Nicola and Alex visited Charlotte Grantham at the nursing home during the next few days. Her progress had been excellent and she was being discharged at the weekend. They had met Mark Benson and liked him, albeit, on Nicola's part, grudgingly. He would appear to have all the characteristics associated with a man of stature and his behaviour in the circumstances could not be faulted. He was a man of thirty, not handsome, or even good-looking, but he had a forceful personality and an air of authority.

It was on the morning before Charlotte was to leave the home, when Nicola's and Alex's visits coincided, neither knowing the other was to be there, that Mark Benson said, as he sat beside the bed to which Charlotte had returned, 'We have a favour to ask.' He looked from Nicola to Alex, aware of the alertness and enquiry on their respective faces.

Charlotte leaned forward in the bed, poised in anticipation as Mark continued, 'Would you, Dr Moncton and Nurse Hardy, be witnesses at our wedding? I've a special licence and it is to be arranged at a register office here in Cheltenham. You have been so kind to us and we want it all to be as quiet as possible.'

Nicola's heart sank. She couldn't think of anything she would dread more. Her gaze went to Alex who was smiling. Obviously he had no qualms. He didn't hesitate as he said, 'I'd be delighted.'

He turned to Nicola, who could only murmur, 'And I.'

She wondered why they hadn't selected their friends, and, as though answering Nicola's unspoken thoughts, Charlotte explained, 'Our closest friends are on holiday and we shall have a little celebration later.' She looked gratefully at Alex. 'I shall never forget your going to see my parents—or how you've supported me these past days. If our request seems almost an impertinence, let our gratitude atone for it.'

Alex assured her that he was honoured to be asked, adding, 'And your parents?'

She said sadly, 'They won't be coming. I've telephoned them. My mother was icy. She made it all so sordid and it upset me. Sister said that I was not to speak to my mother again until I was stronger and back to normal.' Her sigh was deep.

'Sister was right,' Alex said with fervour. 'I see no point in my talking to them again. I'm afraid I should lose my patience.'

'I wouldn't like you to be subjected to that indignity again!' Charlotte exclaimed with feeling.

'What date had you in mind for the wedding?' Alex asked a second or two later.

Mark spoke up. 'We wanted your guidance as to when you felt Charlotte would be fit enough.'

Alex didn't hesitate. 'I'll tell you when she gets home,' he said, looking at Charlotte with a smile. 'I'll obviously want to see you professionally and we can settle matters then.'

'We want to go to Somerset,' Charlotte explained. 'It's near, and will be a honeymoon.' She looked radiant. 'I feel so much better.' She did not pretend even to herself that the loss of the baby had been a tragedy. A child after a year or two of marriage would be better all round. The shock and bereavement of the miscarriage had wounded, but Mark Benson's attitude and devotion had atoned.

'That,' Alex nodded with approval, 'is an excellent idea.' He looked at his watch and said, 'I must go! I've a patient to see...and your lunch is coming in,' he added with a smile as the trolley appeared.

'And I must get back,' Nicola hastened. 'I slipped out during a lull,' she explained, having arrived after Alex.

Alex looked at his patient. 'I'll call at your flat on Sunday morning about eleven,' he promised, 'and let you know when I think you'll be fit enough for the wedding and journey to Somerset.' He looked at Mark Benson. Was he living with his fiancée?

As though reading Alex's thoughts, Mark Benson told them, 'I shall spend the day with Charlotte. I have a flat in the same road.' His gaze was steady. 'We've not decided where we shall live ultimately.'

Alex and Nicola left together.

'A wedding is the last thing I wanted to be drawn into,' Nicola said almost accusingly as she and Alex walked down the long corridor to the exit. She flashed him a somewhat critical look. 'You seemed quite eager to agree to the request.'

'And you didn't hesitate,' he pointed out.

'I had no option.' She added, 'I don't know how we've become involved with them so quickly.' There was a grudging note in her voice and regret in her manner.

Alex looked at her with surprise as he commented, 'Your ringing the hotel. . .you were very helpful.'

Nicola knew that was true and that she often acted impulsively, especially where trouble was concerned.

'Which only goes to show what happens when one acts on impulse.'

'Aren't you building it up out of all proportion because you don't want to, as you say, be drawn into it?'

Her gaze was critical. 'We can't all be as adaptable as you.'

He went straight to the point.

'I don't intend to avoid all weddings because my engagement was broken.'

Nicola lapsed into silence. He always seemed to have the right answer, which made her furious.

He said somewhat irrelevantly, 'I like those two. They have a ring of sincerity about them and are obviously very much in love.'

Nicola tensed. The words stung. She was glad they had reached their respective cars so that further conversation was unnecessary. She didn't respond, but gave her attention to starting the car, and they drove away within seconds of each other. Alex's parting smile was indulgent, as though he assessed her mood.

Julie said on Nicola's return, 'All's been quiet while you've been away. Patient just arrived, though.' She was intrigued by the fact that Dr Alex and Nicola went out together frequently. But there was nothing in

Nicola's manner to suggest any emotional tie. 'Had lunch?' She watched Nicola carefully.

'No. Why?' It was a stupid question, she thought, but there was something that hinted at curiosity in Julie's manner that put her on her guard.

'No reason. I just wondered if you and Dr Alex might——'

Nicola interrupted swiftly.

'Dr Alex is working——'

Julie gave a little laugh.

'All right! Don't bite my head off; you've got that aggressive look about you——'

'And you've got too vivid an imagination,' Nicola countered. She began to walk away and tossed a smile over her shoulder—a smile of conciliation, wondering why she hadn't spontaneously mentioned the wedding. She felt irritated by the fact that Julie had assumed she, Nicola, would have had lunch with Alex. It seemed to impinge on her much valued freedom.

This fact was emphasised that evening when, after Nicola had told her parents of the arrangements, Jan said, 'We wondered if you and Alex would like to come with us to Stratford, to see Ralph Winterton in *Hamlet*?' She spoke lightly, but watched intently, well satisfied with the fact that Alex had been prominently in the picture recently, and hoping to build on it. She was doubly pleased about the wedding, but careful not to stress it since it could only be a delicate subject.

Nicola's momentary silence made Jan add hurriedly, 'We could have dinner and make an evening of it.'

'We're going to Allan and Rosie's one evening,'

Nicola said tentatively, 'but I'm sure Alex would accept your invitation provided he can fit it in.'

Jan smiled. 'Then if you would mention it to him?'

'Very well.' Nicola wasn't enthusiastic, but dismissed the unfair thought that Jan was matchmaking. Going to the theatre at Stratford-upon-Avon had been mentioned the evening Charlotte Grantham had disrupted the proceedings.

Alex said, when told of the suggestion, 'That would be splendid. I haven't seen *Hamlet* for years, and Winterton is considered at his best in the part. And I thoroughly enjoy your parents' company.' He laughed. 'I hope it doesn't lead to another emergency. I don't mind the wedding!' There was a brief pause before he added, 'By the way, we've been invited to the Spencers' garden party at Gloucester Park next week. Saturday. They're——' He stopped, arrested by the resistant expression on Nicola's face, then, 'Why, what's the matter?' His voice held concern.

Her gaze was direct, her voice firm.

'All this socialising,' she protested. 'I don't want us to be regarded as a committed pair.'

CHAPTER SIX

ALEX stared at Nicola aghast, her words stinging and annoying him.

'I don't know when I've done anything to "commit" you,' he retorted harshly.

Nicola didn't retreat from her avowed position.

'The Spencers wouldn't have asked me with you unless our names were associated. Gossip is bound——'

He cut in with faint contempt, '*Gossip*! If doctors took notice of that, they would have to live like monks... *Really*, Nicola!' He paused, his expression suddenly grim. 'If you don't want my company you have only to say so, not think up a ridiculous excuse——'

She rushed in, the memory of his kindness and understanding shaming her. She felt she was behaving badly and allowing thoughts of Stuart too great an influence on her life. It was weak—a fault she despised.

'There's no question of that...' Her voice rose.

'Just that you don't want to be associated with me.' He fought against the annoyance that stabbed and the awareness of her that set his nerves tingling. How obvious it was that she was still in love with Stuart, clinging to the past and rejecting the future.

'I just don't want to create the wrong impression.'

He looked angry. 'Good God! Nicola, even in these days two people can go out together without it being taken for granted that they are lovers.' He held her gaze masterfully. 'I think you have got your emotions into a chaotic state where you cannot see anything in perspective.'

Nicola felt the blood surge into her cheeks. Alex stood there—a challenge that made her feel suddenly inadequate.

'I—I wasn't assuming——'

He interrupted her, 'You just want a little notice pinned on you to say there is nothing whatsoever between us, nor likely to be.' He spoke with cynicism. 'And that you intend to hold the torch *ad infinitum* for the man who let you down. Suppose we face facts.' He was annoyed with himself for being so furious, emotion stabbing as he looked into her large luminous eyes; eyes that met his stormily.

'My feelings are my own concern,' she snapped, wincing because he had touched the edge of the truth, and hastening, 'I value your friendship——' She was making a mess of this and she knew it.

Condescending. The word hit her and she realised he had perceived it as he stared her out and said sharply, almost icily, 'You never need be afraid I shall impose anything more than that on you.' His mouth was grim. 'Or allow anyone else to think that we are a *pair*.' Anger hardened his voice. 'So far as I know there is no question of that, anyway.' His gaze embarrassed her as he added, 'I think you've allowed imagination to run away with you.'

His words stung, yet wasn't his attitude valid?

'I've conveyed the wrong impression,' she mur-

mured, 'but I didn't want people to get the idea——'
She stopped.

'I think you have made yourself perfectly plain,' he emphasised icily, 'and I will tell the Spencers that——'

She protested swiftly, 'I don't want to upset that arrangement; merely to be a little more judicious in future.' It struck her that Julie's remark about lunch had stimulated her ideas and brought home the realisation of how she and Alex were identified. She was immune to the situation from Alex's viewpoint, not realising how self-centred she had become.

'I take it that you are prepared to go to the theatre with your parents and me?' He held her gaze critically.

She looked awkward, but her manner gave assent. Suddenly she wanted to be understood, and rushed on, 'You must see that with us both having had broken engagements, our—our——'

She hesitated and he put in firmly, 'Our *friendship*——'

There was a moment's pause before she exclaimed, 'Yes! Our friendship is naturally a subject for conversation and a matter of conjecture——'

'Neither of which interests me,' he hastened.

Her confusion hardened to resistance.

'Which is where we agree to differ.' The words came forcefully.

He was conscious of her as she stood there, her eyes flashing, her body tense. A feeling of relief surged over her. She did not want to be the subject of gossip; she wanted to be free from involvements and hastily-made friendships which she might afterwards regret. Also, she had the feeling that Alex's friends, having his welfare at heart, would like to see him happily settled, and at the moment she, herself, would be eminently suitable. The possibility appalled her since she craved only freedom from all entanglements.

'We can't very well get out of the wedding,' he said abruptly.

She sighed, her expression uneasy.

'Unfortunately.' She added almost critically, 'Although I'm sure you will enjoy it.'

He stared her out.

'I'm not so jaundiced that I can't enjoy other people's happiness,' he said significantly.

Nicola cringed at the overt rebuke.

'Point taken!' she exclaimed. 'I envy you your *sang froid*. In fact I envy you your whole outlook. Life must be very comfortable.'

He looked away and then directly into her eyes.

'The platitude that life is what we make it is often valid.'

She was outraged and her voice rose as she countered, 'I hardly think that is applicable to either of us, apart from the fact that you almost behave as though a broken engagement is cause for celebration.'

His honesty infuriated her as he retorted, 'In my case I've realised that is a fact.' He added, 'You will not accept that, so it's useless my stressing it.'

Nicola didn't quite know why his sentiments should so annoy her.

'My emotional reaction to life bears no resemblance to yours.'

Her air of confidence was almost intimidating and he found that he wanted to challenge her not with polite argument, but an emotional attack. Not to want to be regarded as a pair indeed! Wasn't she assuming too much, overestimating her power, or the esteem in which she was held? He wanted either to shake her, or kiss her into submission. She stood there, desirable, appealing and infuriating. He could not reach her or press home any advantage, and fell back on a sudden cold inscrutability as he said, 'The fact should suffice where you're concerned.'

He made it sound like a criticism. Yet, when it came to it, couldn't her attitude towards their relationship be near insulting, no matter how logical and valid she might consider it?

And, as though fate were taking a hand, Allan hurried into the room at that juncture, nodding cheerily and saying, 'Is it still all right for Wednesday? We agreed to check.' He shot Alex an enquiring glance. 'Anything wrong? You look a bit grim.' He laughed as he uttered the words and turned to Nicola, who found she was tense as she waited for Alex to speak.

Alex's voice was cold as he addressed her.

'*Is* Wednesday all right for you, or——?'

She hastened, 'Yes,' and was aware of Allan looking anxiously from face to face, then, hearing her acceptance, smiled broadly as he cried, 'Oh, good!' He opened the door and stood with it ajar. 'Give my Mrs Dent a thorough check before she sees me in the morning. I'm afraid we're dealing with Ménière's disease.' This was a group of symptoms all related to damage to the organ of balance—the labyrinth—which was part of the ear.

Nicola didn't hesitate. She relaxed for a second as a

patient came into the conversation, and assured him she would not overlook anything.

Allan nodded, then added irrelevantly, 'We shall have to do some juggling over the Spencers' garden party!' He took it for granted that Alex and Nicola were going.

Nicola heard Alex's voice, crisp and decisive as he said, 'No problem. I shan't be going.'

'But——' Surprise widened Allan's eyes. 'Nicola——' Something in Alex's and Nicola's expression silenced Allan and he mumbled, 'Ah, well. . . Wednesday's all right.' He was gone.

Nicola turned to Alex, her voice reproachful. 'What made you talk of not going to the garden party?'

'I was not "talking", I was making a statement. I can't imagine anything worse than a reluctant guest. It's a very bright affair—quite a highlight.'

Nicola protested, 'You speak as though I'm the only person there is to take. Anyway,' she flashed, 'I didn't suggest not *going*. I——'

'Just not as a *pair*,' he emphasised.

'I was only being honest,' she protested.

'A fact which I've accepted,' he said coldly. 'Let's leave it at that.'

It wasn't as Nicola had foreseen it working out and instead of a feeling of relief she felt bleak.

'Nothing I've said in any way wipes out my appreciation of your kindness.' Her expression was appealing, but it didn't touch him. He was in no mood to placate her, and told himself that he would withdraw from the picture socially and keep their footing on a purely professional basis. He refused to admit to the depression that seeped into him at the turn of events, and decided that she was an impossible person to deal with. Committed as a pair, indeed! She would drive him mad!

It was a perfect September morning when Mark and Charlotte were married. The gold and blue of the day formed a magnificent background for the flowers massed in the Cheltenham gardens. The ceremony was simple and without the austerity of some register offices, the registrar being an understanding, kindly man, who conducted the proceedings with sympathy and dignity, infusing just the right note of solemnity.

Alex had collected Nicola, noticing her powder-blue jacket, crisp white blouse and skirt. She looked subdued but striking, and she lowered her gaze from his, aware of his lightweight grey suit and white shirt and his somewhat withdrawn air as he greeted her. The evening with Allan and Rosie had been low-key and the old spontaneity had vanished.

Now as they stood together in the rather bare office—aware of the radiant bride in a soft mauve crêpe dress which emphasised her excellent figure, standing proudly beside her husband-to-be—they exchanged a significant glance that held memories of what might have been, and tension mounted.

Nicola reflected that, had the circumstances been different, Stuart would have been with her, and her eyes misted as memory stabbed. What was Alex thinking? No doubt congratulating himself that he had escaped the tie; certainly he would not be experiencing any heartache. She felt his gaze upon her again and looked away—and in that moment Alex felt emotion surge and his heart seem to stop beating.

'I now pronounce you man and wife.' The utterance held the promise of triumph; the atmosphere tensed as the newly married couple looked into each other's eyes.

And in that second Alex knew that he was in love with Nicola; that he would give all he possessed if she could be his wife. It didn't matter that she infuriated him, that she had made it abundantly clear she didn't want to be emotionally associated with him and was obviously still in love with Stuart; he was bound to her by a bond nothing could break and if he obeyed his instinct he would have taken her in his arms and kissed her into submission. As it was, from then on he avoided looking at her and concentrated solely upon the newly-weds. When all the formalities were over, they stood outside the building beside Mark's car, their happiness evident for all to see as they were about to set off on their journey to Somerset and what was to be an idyllic honeymoon.

'Thank you for completing our happiness on this day,' Charlotte said in parting.

Mark seconded that, and Alex was very grateful there was not to be a meal or any outward celebration, in order that they might reach Bath for lunch, making it their centre from which they could explore the surrounding countryside. Charlotte was a graphic artist with a local company and had managed to get an extended holiday on health grounds. Mark was his own master and had arranged the break without trouble.

Nicola's gaze was drawn to the wedding-ring on Charlotte's hand. How often she had visualised one on hers, and how bare her third finger seemed at that moment. Even as she diverted her gaze she realised that Alex was watching her, his expression hard. They stood together as the happy couple drove away with last farewells, and he might have been a stranger.

Nicola's nearness was a torment and the irony of the situation reduced Alex to silence as he opened the door of the car and saw her into the passenger-seat. He was aware that she had a baffled air about her, but neither was able to break the tense silence until he said as they had almost reached the Park, 'Thank God for work.'

She resented his attitude and said the wrong thing. 'Marriages evidently don't agree with you, despite your outlook. I'm surprised.' Her voice was edgy.

He shot at her, 'You're not very good at assessing my feelings, while making your own abundantly clear.' He wanted to shout at her, make her realise that her ultimatum about their relationship was like a death knell to his hopes, but he knew that a wrong move would be fatal and the only wise course was to be withdrawn and emotionally disinterested. She wanted space, he told himself for the dozenth time; she should have it. It was the only card to play. Yet if he were to follow that tactic, wasn't it essential that he behave with near indifference rather than aggression? Aggression begged emotion, whereas indifference brought stalemate, while stimulating conjecture.

'I do not need to assess your feelings,' she retorted, 'only to weigh up your actions.'

'Isn't the one a reflection of the other?' The question was abrupt.

'Not always; events can sweep one along and one finds oneself in a situation against one's will.'

'I don't need reminding of that where you are concerned.' His voice hardened. 'We've settled that issue, Nicola. We'll call it a day with the theatre outing. I would not like to let your parents down. Ironical that we have to wait another ten days for the seats.'

There was an air of finality in his manner that went beyond her initial idea. Yet, as against that, she felt a sense of relief that she was no longer tied to being squired to engagements where she was always identified with him and thus denied freedom. After her experience with Stuart, freedom seemed a panacea, and she intended to enjoy it. Seriously to have her name associated with another man was the very last thing she wanted and she wondered if she would ever regain her trust in the opposite sex, or find any sexual stimulation in their company. Her mood changed and her spirits lifted. The wedding was over, the depression of anticipating the event gone. Nothing Alex could say, she argued, would upset her now. She congratulated herself on having established a stable pattern for the future. It had taken her a considerable time to come to terms with events and establish a formula.

Alex didn't speak as he stopped the car and politely came round to her side, by which time she had half stepped out on to the pavement. He cupped her elbow, aware of her nearness and wanting to draw her into his arms. Instead, he stood back formally and they went into the reception hall together, his expression mask-like.

Julie said, 'Mrs Drayton has an appointment this afternoon, Dr Alex.' She gave the name significance.

Alex frowned. Mrs Drayton was the practice nightmare who always had some imaginary complaint that dared not be ignored. She had a crush on Alex and had done her best to manoeuvre him into her circle of friends, without success, much to the irritation of her husband, who knew to this regret that she was a difficult, immature woman who strove at all times to have her own way.

'Why?' he asked bluntly.

Julie looked at him, trying to conceal a smile.

'A lump in her breast that she discovered last night.'

It was always something that required an examination.

Nicola looked at Alex. She had no idea why, in that moment, she remembered he was her doctor and all that entailed.

His gaze was professional, his voice clipped, as he addressed her.

'Arrange to attend me when the examination is taking place.' He implied that, if she kept any patient waiting, so be it.

'Very well.'

Julie said, 'Mrs Latimer would like a word with you.'

Alex, preoccupied, nodded, but didn't look at Nicola as he walked away.

'Good wedding?' Julie asked as he was out of earshot.

'Very.'

Julie inclined her head in Alex's direction. 'Mrs

Drayton is all he was short of. She must know every ailment in the medical dictionary. *Not* his type.'

'What,' scoffed Nicola, 'is anyone's type, when you think of the mess half of us make of our affairs?'

Julie looked complacent. 'I'm very satisfied with my life at the moment, thank you very much.'

'Good for you.' Nicola infused a note of congratulations into her voice. 'What time this afternoon is Mrs Drayton coming?'

'Three.'

Nicola sighed, nodded and went to her room.

Mrs Drayton came into Alex's consulting-room in a wave of expensive perfume and wearing a black *couture* jacket and skirt. She was a pretty woman with china-blue eyes and a pink and white complexion; thirty, slim. Her husband was a rich acquisition whom she dominated for no better reason than he liked to be seen with a wife who always looked immaculate and in the height of fashion, and who ran an excellent and attractive house.

Nicola watched Alex's face as Julie showed the patient into his consulting-room. He had said little before her arrival and merely flicked through her extensive case notes, giving an impatient sigh. Now he held out his hand in a welcome he was far from feeling.

Mrs Drayton said in a faintly pathetic voice, 'I'm so sorry to worry you again so soon, Dr Moncton, but I'm so *worried*. . . I mean finding the lump was such a shock——'

Alex interrupted her with all the patience he could muster, allowing for the fact that, while he had examined her breasts many times, there could nevertheless be the one dread occasion when the result was positive.

'Let's have a look at you.' He spoke encouragingly as he handed over to Nicola, who led the way into the examining-room, while Alex watched with seeming concern until the door closed behind them.

Mrs Drayton was always frustrated that a nurse should be there. She wanted to see Dr Moncton alone; to be able to talk intimately to him and get to know him at a different level. There was something fascinatingly withdrawn about him that increased the attraction. She said in a breath as she and Nicola reached the examining couch, 'Dr Moncton is such an understanding, sympathetic man. It must be very rewarding to work for him.'

Nicola merely inclined her head and said, 'Just take off your clothes to the waist.'

Mrs Drayton did as she was asked, sliding down an exquisite lace-trimmed slip and bra, and getting on the examining couch with an experienced gesture.

Nicola immediately drew the sheet up to cover what the patient knew to be perfectly shaped breasts.

Alex joined them and began his examination. Nicola stood sentinel as his hands went delicately and dextrously over the whole area.

Mrs Drayton's thoughts were unruly. She was conscious of Alex's nearness, his touch; she could smell the faint doctor smell that was part of his surroundings and wondered what it would be like to be made love to by him. To be told that he loved her, wanted her; and conscious of her quickening heartbeat she said emphatically, to regain control, 'The lump was near the nipple.'

Alex gave her a thorough examination, only speaking when he had instructions to give, and then stood back, a confident expression on his face. 'There is no lump; no adhesions and no sign of mastitis, Mrs Drayton.' Nicola had pulled the sheet up again and felt that the patient had lost a little of her power.

'But——'

Alex's voice hardened. 'You are absolutely clear.'

Nicola caught his eye and knew his mood.

'Help Mrs Drayton to dress, Nurse, and bring her into my room,' he said authoritatively and, without another word, left them.

Mrs Drayton flushed and looked a little flustered. She felt that she had gone too far and, humiliatingly, Dr Moncton had been aware of the fact. A rather sick, miserable feeling stole over her; she could see her visits dwindling to nothing and the thought made her desperate.

'Do you get many false alarms?' Her voice shook as she addressed Nicola.

Nicola wanted subtly to warn her against wasting Alex's time.

'Quite a few. We are more concerned with those who put off coming through fear.'

Mrs Drayton flushed again.

'I—I was terrified!' she said dramatically.

Nicola just looked at her and could not help saying, 'I am sure you would never avoid seeking advice, Mrs Drayton.' She had no general conversation with this woman and felt irritated by her, wondering what her next visit would be in aid of.

'Dr Moncton is always insistent that I should come to see him if ever I am worried about anything.'

Nicola would like to have said, 'Yes; but not the finger ache, and if you think you can fool him you are much mistaken.'

Alex looked Mrs Drayton straight in the eye a few minutes later as he said, 'You can congratulate yourself, Mrs Drayton: you are a perfectly healthy woman. I have examined you at different times and would have no hesitation in giving you a clean bill of health.'

She looked crestfallen. Her last prop had been taken away and she could not plunge into conversation of a social nature.

She made a last effort. 'I don't always feel well and you told me that if ever anything was worrying——' She broke off.

Alex felt that he had established his point and could not take it further, so was forced to reply with pleasant authority, 'I am your doctor, always here in any emergency, of course.' His smile quickened her heartbeat. 'And now,' he hurried on, 'if you'll excuse me, I have another patient to see.'

Mrs Drayton's hand clung to his in parting; she met his gaze and her own was intense. The thought flashed wildly through her mind that if she were to become pregnant she would at least see him on a permanent basis and there would be several months before her appearance was noticeably changed. If only he would give her some indication that he found her seductive, or that she represented more than just a patient.

Nicola saw her out and returned to Alex, saying a

trifle ridiculingly, 'There's one patient, among many, who has an outsize crush on you.'

He cringed. 'Don't!'

Nicola persisted, without quite knowing why, aware of his discomfiture, 'You know it's true.' It struck her that at least she had never fallen into that category, or concentrated on Alex's charms, having no time for women who regarded their respective doctors as film stars. She added in a conciliatory tone, 'Not surprising that doctors get struck off: they have more than enough temptation.'

Alex was roused as he protested, 'I find such patients irritating and pathetic.'

'Nevertheless you handle them expertly.' She studied him with interest, finding herself assessing him through the eyes of the obsessed.

'I am their doctor,' he said bluntly. 'Just that.' His lips set into a firm line.

Nicola gave a little laugh as she said lightly, 'Considered by all to be very charming.'

He wanted to assert, 'Except by you,' and was overwhelmed once again with the desire to take her in his arms and feel her lips and body yielding to his. Instead, he commented with faint cynicism, 'The medical profession is the centre of criticism and conjecture.' He added without quite knowing why, 'I'm sure you have no illusions about it.'

Their gaze was deep and steady as she replied, 'I am more than satisfied with my doctor.' Her words came deliberately.

He glanced away from her and idly moved a letter on

his desk before looking up and saying unexpectedly, 'Provided he never forgets that he *is* your doctor.'

There was a faint pause before she said smoothly, 'Naturally.'

Alex tensed; his expression hardened as he flicked down the intercom and said to Julie, 'Send in the next patient.'

Nicola accepted her dismissal. Nothing more was said as she immediately went from the room.

Alex sat at his desk and held his head in his hands, staring in the direction she had gone.

It was one thing to decide to give her space, but quite another to carry it out.

CHAPTER SEVEN

NICOLA had no idea what the pattern of her relationship with Alex would be after that scene, but was not prepared for his formal detached manner during the few weeks that followed, when September slid into October and russet and gold took the place of green. Work was their only contact with the exception of the visit to the theatre, with its splendid auditorium and air of elegance. She had sat next to him, noticing his remote politeness while aware that her parents were conscious of the atmosphere and a little bewildered by it.

To Alex her nearness, the occasional brushing of arms, the fragrant warmth of her body, were a form of exquisite torture and it took every scrap of his self-control to maintain a cool, pleasant attitude, without appearing ungracious to Timothy and Jan. He wanted to reach out and clasp Nicola's hands as they lay in her lap; to whisper, 'I love you,' and end the suspense and torment of her coldness. The shadow of Stuart lay between them and he felt that she was not listening to the play, but riveted to the past when no doubt she had sat with Stuart in that same theatre.

'You don't,' he said in an interval when they remained in their seats, 'seem to be enjoying the evening.' It was a deliberate observation, and Timothy and Jan exchanged surprised glances.

She turned a cool gaze upon him. 'There is such a thing as knowing a play too well—even Shakespeare.'

'Or a person,' Alex added and stared her out. He knew the moment he had uttered the words that they were unwise.

Her voice was clipped. 'Better than not knowing them at all.'

Silence fell. Even Jan could not cut through the tension. She and Timothy had agreed that they would play a part in bringing Alex and Nicola together and create social occasions in which they might both partake, but this beginning seemed a disaster. They were at a loss to understand why the former *bonhomie* was missing and Nicola was so obviously cool. Equally, they both knew that she distanced herself from any close association and therefore they must tread carefully, not allowing their thankfulness that Stuart was out of the picture to overrule discretion in their desire to see Alex in her life, their regard for him as strong as their respect and admiration.

Not even the terrific ovation at the end of the play roused Nicola from her depression, or struck a note of brightness. She was aware of Alex's tall figure beside her as they struggled through the crowd on their way out of the theatre. She glanced up at him, but there was no recognition in his eyes, which were staring ahead as though he were miles away.

When invited back for a drink, Alex was grateful for the genuine excuse that he had arranged to be on call after the theatre. Nicola thought he made the declaration with a degree of satisfaction, reminding herself that he was taking her at her word and keeping his part of the bargain. Her heart felt heavy. The theatre! Stuart, and drinks afterwards. . .

Her mother's voice broke into her reverie. They were home and having a brandy, Nicola remaining in their sitting-room as a gesture of appreciaton for the evening, although she was in no mood for conversation.

Jan said boldly, her gaze direct, 'Alex was right, Nicola.'

'In what way?' Nicola tensed.

'You didn't seem to enjoy the evening. I'm sorry.'

Nicola was surprised at Jan's directness. She had been very discreet thus far and only on rare occasions made the general situation an issue.

'I'm sorry if I seemed ungracious,' she hastened. 'No accounting for moods.'

Timothy didn't mince matters. 'I'd like to see you settle into a happier one.'

Nicola was roused.

'Meaning that I'm a bore.' She went on, 'I don't have to pretend to Alex. I've made my intentions quite plain to him. I'm weary of socialising. Going around in circles is not my idea of pleasure. It's all so artificial.'

'There's no virtue in isolation,' Timothy said bluntly, but his expression was anxious.

Nicola relented.

'I'm being ungracious!' she exclaimed. 'It was good of you to arrange this evening. I've been a wet blanket, I'm afraid.' She gave a little apologetic laugh. 'Not in the mood for Shakespeare, perhaps.' She added directly, 'Stuart and I saw quite a few of his plays together and one doesn't forget.' She uttered the words a little belligerently, resisting the fact that everyone was willing, even expecting her to forget Stuart and make a fresh start. The logic was not lost on her, but she seemed incapable of facing the future with hope and a belief that happiness would be restored to her. She felt, too, that Alex was losing—if he had not already lost—patience with her, and the fact engendered a bleak depression for which she despised herself. She wanted life on her own terms, yet was not certain exactly what those terms were, dissatisfied with any circumstances that prevailed.

Jan looked at her very directly. 'You evidently didn't see the announcement of Stuart's marriage in the local paper last evening.' She had avoided mentioning it, but suddenly felt that it was appropriate to do so and, thus, close the chapter.

Nicola started; her heartbeat quickened. She faced up to the finality.

'No,' she admitted, and there was a note of cynicism in her voice. Had Alex seen it?

She asked him the following day when they had a few minutes alone together, without knowing why she should bring him into it.

He felt an immediate sense of relief which showed in his expression.

'I hope that enables you to see the past in perspective,' he said firmly. 'If you could just wish them happiness, the past would fade.' He added, 'I hadn't seen the announcement.'

She looked at him with faint criticism tinged with irritation. 'You have a very convenient philosophy. I certainly don't wish them ill. I hope I'm not *so* small-minded.' Her voice shook. 'Is your opinion of me so low?'

His heart was racing. He longed to make love to her as she stood close to him, her face raised to his, forlorn, tempting; and suddenly he pressed his lips to hers in a shattering kiss as he penetrated the warm softness of her mouth, then, shocked, drew back almost before she had time to reject him, or respond.

'I'm sorry,' he murmured hoarsely.

She stood there shaking, not having been kissed by any man since Stuart left her, and to overcome emotion she said sharply, 'You have obviously forgotten that you are my doctor. Or do you regard me as a patient who needs comforting?'

Desire flooded through him as he fought against the passion aroused by the sensuousness of her lips. Nevertheless there was compassion in the look he gave her and she flared up at what she considered his pity, her eyes flashing as she cried, 'I don't want an *apology*——'

Emotion stabbed him into retaliation. 'What *do* you want——?' He stopped, the question foolish and empty as he thought bitterly that only one name—*Stuart*—answered the question.

She stared at him, suddenly subdued, not wanting to be reminded of the past by a kiss that had no meaning and merely emphasised his pity, which had obviously been instrumental in his behaving out of character.

'Suppose we forget the incident,' she said with finality. Her gaze met his and she was aware of his withdrawn expression which made him almost a stranger.

Alex dared not trust himself to speak and his silence

gave assent. He was acutely conscious of her as she stood there, a challenge and a temptation he could barely resist. But he knew that a wrong move now would be fatal; that he had come near to wrecking their relationship and must tread carefully if he was to retain her confidence. '*Forget the incident.*' He knew that it would haunt him, leaving him forever on the edge of desire.

Nicola changed her mood deliberately, sliding into a safe professionalism.

'Mrs Brent popped in to see me this morning. She thinks she's pregnant.'

Mrs Brent, thirty-two, was a favourite patient who had been hoping for a child ever since her marriage three years previously, and had endured two false alarms.

Nicola added hurriedly, 'I made an appointment for you to see her this afternoon.'

Alex was immediately interested.

'Let's hope it will be third time lucky. The Brents are a fine couple and could give a child a happy home.' His voice was warm and enthusiastic.

Despite herself, Nicola thought what a humane, sympathetic man he was, involved with his patients and their problems. She nodded. A little sick sensation of envy stole over her.

He looked solemn. 'If she shows any untoward symptoms, I shall advise bed rest.'

There was an easy atmosphere as he spoke, the tension gone. Each in turn was considering the patient's interests.

Nicola exclaimed, 'That would be possible in her

case! She has that rare boon of living-in help by way of her old nanny. . .but she may not be pregnant.'

Their eyes met in understanding.

'It's rewarding to be involved,' he said, his voice sympathetic.

Nicola spoke involuntarily. 'That is what makes you such a good doctor—you are always involved.'

He raised his eyebrows and looked surprised, as though a compliment from her was the last thing he expected.

'Thank you,' he said quietly. 'It is not supposed to be a good thing, but I can't treat case notes.'

An understanding silence fell, taking the place of the thunder of a few minutes before. Once again, Nicola was reminded of his basic kindness and compassion. She thought of his kiss and her reaction to it, realising it had left a reminder that all physical demonstration had gone from her world. She recalled Alex's words about wishing Stuart and his wife happiness, and seeing life in perspective again. If only it were as simple as that.

'My next patient is due,' he said formally, the atmosphere suddenly changing. 'Would you be good enough to tell Julie to wait a few minutes before showing her in? I've a telephone call to make.'

Nicola moved quickly to the door. He went to his desk. A shutter might have come down between them. Alex's control was at an end.

Nicola saw Alex later, after Mrs Brent's appointment. Mrs Brent had looked in on Nicola, having seen Alex, and excitedly proclaimed the news that she *was* pregnant.

'About nine weeks,' he said, adding, 'She had some kind of superstition about coming to me too early. I shall have to watch her like a hawk.'

Nicola felt a tug at her heart—a mixture of personal regret at her own position and anxiety for the patient.

'She's a very attractive woman,' she said irrelevantly.

Alex stiffened.

'I fail to see what that has to do with it.'

'Perhaps not; but don't you think she's attractive?'

Alex frowned. 'My only concern is seeing that the pregnancy goes to term successfully.'

Nicola stared him out as she said, 'You'll be a great comfort to her, whether you find her attractive or not.' The words rushed out. 'Your speciality is comforting people.'

'You make it sound like a fault.'

And in that second his kiss lay between them as a dangerous symbol.

She didn't lower her gaze as she almost challenged him, 'Only if you *know* it to be a weakness that complicates your relationships.'

Alex wanted to take her in his arms and tell her how greatly *she* complicated their relationship, and what restraint was imposed upon him to maintain their present friendship. He knew that he must avoid intimate discussions and treat her with cool pleasantness which would negate the kiss and give her the space she demanded.

'I'm in no mood for psychological discussions,' he said firmly and on a faint note of authority.

Nicola's voice had an edge to it. 'The practice nurse will return to her job.'

And with that she left his room before he had time to say anything further.

Julie hailed her in the reception area. 'Hi! What's wrong?'

Nicola started and echoed the word, 'Wrong?'

'You look grim!'

'Nonsense. . . I'm looking forward to having supper with you and Barry tonight.'

Julie wondered if the news of Stuart's marriage was responsible for Nicola's mood, but was sufficiently tactful not to mention the fact. On the other hand it had not escaped her that Nicola had been frequently in Dr Alex's company recently. But it was difficult, she decided, to fathom Nicola's reactions.

It was a happy evening spent at Barry's flat, where Julie had prepared an excellent buffet. Nicola told herself that it was pleasant to be on her own, with just the two of them, and the word *freedom* caught at her imagination. She was glad that Alex's name had not been mentioned and no emotional problems intruded into the conversation. Barry was a slim, tall young man of twenty-eight, who was quite capable of looking after himself in the modern fashion. He had wanted to cook a meal, but had settled for Julie's idea of a buffet. She hadn't any facilities for entertaining at her bed-sit. He and Nicola got on very well on the few occasions they had met and she liked his frank, clear eyes and cheerful expression. She resisted the summing-up that he was a man one could trust.

It was when they were drinking their wine and almost at the end of the meal that Julie said, 'We've some news to tell you.'

A strange feeling of apprehension stole over Nicola. That probably meant they were going to live together.

But Julie said, almost proudly, 'Barry and I are going to be married.'

Nicola started and her heart sank. For a second there was a tense silence, which she broke by saying, 'That's splendid! I hope you will be very happy.'

They looked at each other, smiled, clasped hands and Julie said, 'Thank you; we shall.'

Julie had pondered over the method by which she should tell Nicola of the event, not wanting to rub salt into a wound, yet arguing that Nicola would have to face up to the real world eventually and not be cushioned against hurt indefinitely, or she would never recover from her own disillusionment.

Nicola uttered one word. 'When?'

She hung on the reply, unable to explain why she hoped it would not be soon.

'As soon as the banns have been read—at St Mary's, the parish church off the High Street.'

Nicola sat very still. She had nothing to say, but her thoughts raced. Instinctively she didn't want to attend and hoped it was going to be a quiet affair.

As though reading her thoughts, Julie explained, 'We shall have it early in the morning, with only our closest friends and parents there.' She paused. 'You and Dr Alex, of course.'

Nicola tensed.

'I can't speak for him,' she said abruptly.

Julie was not lost to the tone of voice and asked herself if she had been correct in taking it for granted that there was something building up between Dr Alex and Nicola, although Nicola had certainly seemed irascible after leaving his room that morning.

Barry spoke up, 'Do doctors usually attend the weddings of their staff?'

Julie was enthusiastic. 'Dr Alex would. He's not a bit stand-offish.' She added deliberately, 'I shall hope to be invited to his wedding, that's for sure!'

Nicola gasped involuntarily, '*His* wedding?'

'Yes,' Julie said emphatically. 'I can't wait for the right woman to come along and snap him up. She'll be very lucky.' She stared Nicola out. 'Don't you agree?'

Nicola hedged, 'He is a very kind man.'

'And not in the least bitter.' Julie wanted to draw Nicola out and make Alex a subject for conversation, but felt Nicola's instinctive resistance in her qualified comment. Kind was a very safe word, and, while it bore testimony to the truth, it lacked all the vitality and sex appeal that Julie associated with Alex.

Nicola relived Alex's kiss and the scene that followed it. She could read Julie's thoughts and wanted to emphasise that there would be no question of her being escorted to the wedding by Alex, as had obviously been in Julie's mind. Now, more than ever, she was glad she had taken her stand and left Alex in no doubt that she wanted complete freedom. It was important to establish the fact with Julie.

Nicola looked at Julie very levelly. 'Implying that I am bitter?' Her voice was quiet and enquiring. She glanced at Barry, half apologising for the trend of the conversation.

Julie, having built up a romance between Alex and Nicola and hoping to further it, cried, 'Why, no!'

Nicola relaxed and smiled as she said, 'Now that you two have found happiness, don't imagine that I have any desire to follow in your footsteps.' She paused before adding, 'All I ask is to be left alone to enjoy my freedom. I don't want to be associated with anyone, so don't conjure up any possible suitors for my own good!' She laughed, but there was no mirth within her. 'So now you know. Romance and I have nothing in common, and that's the way I want it.'

Julie looked serious and was about to protest when Nicola said firmly, 'I trust you to take me at my word.'

The subject was dropped and with it went some of the spontaneity of the conversation.

Nicola left the flat a little early, feeling a hollow emptiness as she reached home and, not wanting to be alone, went into Timothy and Jan's sitting-room where they were having a nightcap. They didn't express any surprise at her appearance.

Timothy indicated his brandy glass. 'Join us?'

Nicola endeavoured to put a note of brightness into her voice.

'A small one.' She smiled and settled in a deep armchair, saying without preliminaries, 'Julie and Barry are going to be married.'

Jan's reaction was immediate.

'Oh! Good.'

'Only met Barry once,' Timothy said, 'but I liked him.'

Nicola's thoughts raced; she could never disabuse herself of the idea that, when it came to it, her parents had not really been keen on Stuart, even though the fact had not manifested itself until after the engagement was broken.

'A snap judgement,' she challenged.

Jan changed the subject and after a few minutes of general discussion said, 'Alex came in this evening.'

Nicola's eyes widened. She looked surprised. It so happened that he knew she would not be there and the fact emphasised the gap between them.

'Really.' It was an indifferent sound.

'We're going to dinner with him and his father next week,' Timothy put in.

Nicola gave a little gasp and, aware of the stupidity of the observation, said, 'But you've never met his father.'

Jan laughed.

'There's no law against our doing so!'

Nicola looked confused. Obviously she, herself, was not to be invited or she would have been included. Her thoughts were in turmoil. Perhaps Alex intended asking her himself. She made up her mind in advance that she would not go, arguing that to make it a family affair would subtly avoid any twosome which she had so vehemently denigrated. She decided that Alex would prove to be a stubborn adversary.

Timothy and Jan had been pleased with the invitation, since it would provide them with an opportunity of returning the hospitality and thus create a further occasion for Alex and Nicola to meet socially. They were unashamedly desirous for their relationship to deepen and had been well satisfied by their recent socialising, not wanting it to lessen, aware that Nicola's attitude had momentarily changed and that she had gone back into her shell.

Jan said spontaneously, 'I thought we'd give a Hallowe'en party.'

Timothy laughed.

'What has that got to do with our going to dinner with Alex and his father?'

'Nothing! But we haven't done much entertaining lately and it's time we started again.' She looked at Nicola as if to say, 'We don't want you clinging to yesterday just because Stuart is married.'

Nicola tensed. She could read her mother's thoughts and was well aware of the fact that Jan sensed a change in her attitude.

'You are,' she said lightly, 'in the happy position of being able to do as you please and fill the flat if you wish!'

'Meaning that the idea doesn't appeal to you?' Jan watched her carefully.

'As long as I do not have to be connected with any one person, the more the merrier,' Nicola said brightly, but there was a warning note behind the assertion of which her parents were aware. She looked from face to face. 'As you know, I've seen the announcement, so you don't have to worry. I've adjusted to things and know precisely where I'm going.' She added with a smile, 'I've also come to the conclusion that it would be a good idea to go to Switzerland this winter and learn to ski. Something quite new and exciting. I haven't been in the mood to think of holidays recently, which reminds me: you haven't been away, either.' It struck her, even as she spoke, how completely self-centred she'd been.

Jan said, too hastily, 'We haven't wanted to bother.'

Nicola gave a significant grunt.

'Then think of doing so now,' she countered emphatically.

Timothy said with what Jan knew was deliberation, 'Oddly enough, Alex was talking of taking a break this autumn.'

Nicola started. Alex was full of surprises, she thought, and wondered why he hadn't mentioned the fact to her. As against that, what possible encouragement had she given him to do so? Most certainly there would not be any more compassionate kisses and their understanding of each other was exemplary inasmuch as they would never see eye to eye, and accepted the fact.

Nevertheless after she had gone through her case notes with him the following morning, she found herself wondering if he would make any reference to his visit to her parents the previous evening, or suggest that she join in the dinner invitation. There was nothing in his manner to betray his feelings. His gaze met hers very levelly, giving no hint of the admiration he felt for her as she stood there in her uniform, looking smart and at the same time sensuous. Emotion lay just beneath the surface and, in turn, Nicola had to admit that the general opinion of him as an attractive man was valid. He had a certain magnetism, a personality which could not be ignored. She took the qualities for granted and emphasised the fact that he had proved to be a sympathetic friend, ready to accept her terms.

Alex meanwhile had visited her parents, wishing to establish and deepen the friendship by availing himself of their hospitality and returning it, irrespective of Nicola, so that she would enjoy space and freedom from him, without his fading from the picture. His love and desire for her were too great to allow him to retreat without a fight, so that it became a question of tactics. He deliberately didn't mention her parents and she told herself again that she was infinitely relieved that the change in their relationship had taken place so smoothly.

Their conversation was purely professional until, when the meeting was about to end, she said abruptly, 'Have you heard that Julie and Barry are going to be married?'

'Yes. Julie told me when I came in this morning.' His voice was smooth, his expression interested. 'She has looked very happy lately.'

Nicola felt irritated. He had a knack of always associating marriages and engagements with happiness.

'You're very observant.'

He smiled. 'My job to be.'

'If she doesn't look happy now, when will she?' Nicola wanted to be difficult.

He didn't rise to the bait.

'I shall go to their wedding.' He seemed to emphasise the singular. 'Thank heaven Julie is not contemplating leaving us.'

So! Julie had already invited him to the great occasion.

'Do you usually attend the weddings of members of your staff?' The words came out jerkily. Her gaze was direct.

Alex laughed. 'That suggests we have a large staff.'

Nicola flushed. It was a silly question.

'But,' he went on as though to placate her, 'we have had two marriages—receptionists in the past—and yes, I did attend them.'

'No practice nurses?' It was a cynical utterance.

He held her gaze and robbed her of her nerve as he said pointedly, 'No. . . I'll wait for yours.'

'Then you will wait forever.'

The silence that fell was electric.

CHAPTER EIGHT

IT WAS the following evening before Alex and Nicola saw each other again. It had been a hectic day with several emergencies that had necessitated home visits and Alex had been out quite a bit of the time. They met in the entrance hall.

'The first peaceful moment I've had today,' Alex said, wanting to invite her out for a meal while knowing it would be a fatal move.

'My day hasn't been exactly restful either,' she confessed, adding, 'I hope you've got a free evening.'

Nothing could have established the distance between them more than the conversational remark and he was not lost to it.

'With luck, yes.' He held her gaze as he added, 'I shall look in on Harry and Sue.'

Nicola remembered the Sunday lunch with them and how, on their subsequent meetings, she had always been aware of their hope that they might be told of an engagement. Even their thoughts had seemed noisy. She deliberately didn't send any message. A little while previously his 'free evening' would have included her. She moved towards the front door which, it being October, was closed.

'I'm looking forward to luxuriating with a PD James book,' she said brightly and, without realising it, deliberately.

He moved swiftly and opened the door.

Somewhat absently she went outside, their gaze meeting for a split second before she gave a piercing cry as she fell headlong down the steps to the pavement below.

Alex, horrified, reached her and knelt beside her twisted body, calling her name, when the words, 'My darling,' nearly escaped his lips.

Nicola murmured foolishly, 'So. . .sorry.' She indicated her ribs and right knee, both having banged against the edge of the second and fourth steps. Her stocking was ripped, the knee bleeding and grazed.

Alex crouched beside her and cradled her in his arms. She winced at the movement and let him take the weight of her body. She was white and struggling not to make a fuss as she murmured, 'My ribs——' The pain was excruciating and it hurt her to breathe. She looked up at him forlornly. 'How could I be so *foolish*——?' The words came with difficulty and she let her head fall back on his shoulder, feeling faint.

Alex was making rapid calculations. She would have to be X-rayed, to make sure there was no internal damage and that a broken rib had not pierced the lung.

'I'm going to take you straight to the Cotswold,' he said gently. 'It will be better to get you into my car than to manoeuvre you back up the steps.'

Nicola struggled to straighten herself and managed to stretch her left leg, realising it was undamaged and mobile at the knee. She moved from his arms and was able to manage a sitting position.

Alex supported her by her elbows, her head against his chest. As he did so, their eyes met and she was touched by the concern, anxiety and sympathy that lay in his expression. She was thankful for his presence and the fact that he was her doctor, prepared for him to be wholly in charge as she murmured, 'Whatever you say. . . My parents. . .'

'I'll get you into the car and then alert my father. He'll take care of the details.'

Nicola nodded. Her head was aching and she felt slightly giddy. Two neighbours hurried towards them, anxious to help, retrieving Nicola's handbag, which lay on the pavement. With a series of dextrous movements and their help, Alex got her into the front seat of the Volvo, which was roomy with excellent leg space. She could not stay the little groan as she sat down and the aching pain worsened. She let her head fall back against the headrest and looked at Alex with grateful apology.

'Such a nuisance,' she gasped.

He put a hand over hers as they lay in her lap. His touch was soothing and made words unnecessary. The thought went through her mind of how infinitely kind he was, no matter what the emergency. It did not occur to her to protest about going to the nursing home, content to leave the decisions in his hands.

'I won't be more than a minute or two,' Alex promised. He assessed her with a professional gaze, spoke to the two helpful neighbours who remained, and then hurried up the steps and into the house.

Nicola closed her eyes, swimming in a sea of pain, lost to her surroundings until she heard Alex say, 'Everything's taken care of. I spoke to Jan. . .' the car moved as he talked, his voice was low '. . .and to the nursing home.'

'I don't want to stay there.'

'Depends on what the X-rays show. I'm not having you take any chances.' There was authority in his manner. 'And don't forget that I'm in charge,' he added.

She managed to murmur, 'Yes, Doctor.'

Alex's emotions were very near the surface. He felt anything but her doctor as he sat there, hating to see her suffering, wanting to comfort her and tell her of his love, while knowing that this was not the right time. He must live up to his position, remember his professional responsibilities and not take advantage of the temptation of the situation, or her vulnerability at the moment.

Alex was cordially received at the Cotswold, where Charlotte Grantham had been treated prior to her marriage to Mark Benson, and, curiously enough, even at the dramatic moment of Nicola's arrival there the thought of Charlotte flashed through her mind. Fate, Nicola reflected. Now here *she* was, at the same nursing home, in Alex's care.

A trolley was brought immediately after Alex went through the main entrance and gave an order. Nicola was aware of his arm about her shoulders as he and the porter eased her out of the car and lifted her on to the trolley, but as she attempted to lie back she gave an agonised gasp and said painfully, 'Not lie down.'

'I'll get a chair,' the porter said immediately, moving swiftly.

Alex supported Nicola's shoulders, his body taking the weight as he stood close to her. She was conscious of his nearness, relaxing thankfully against him.

A few minutes later the porter wheeled her into the large reception area of the nursing home, where a vast desk filled the right-hand side of one wall, with two receptionists manning the telephones while two nurses were giving instructions and greeting the patients. But even as they moved over the threshold a dark-haired attractive sister quickly came towards them.

'Why, Dr Moncton!' Her voice was anxious as she looked at Nicola with a degree of concerned enquiry.

'Sister Adams!' Alex said warmly. He added hurriedly, 'I hoped you might be on duty.' He made the necessary introductions and explained the circumstances. 'I want Nurse Hardy X-rayed. . .and her knee attended to. Is Dr Mason about?'

'His team is on emergency X-rays this evening. . . you're lucky.' Nurse Adams knew that the two men were friends.

Nicola had only a blurred impression of the events that followed. The knee being examined; the pain of being undressed and put into a white gown; the dark eeriness of the X-ray room with its futuristic machines and momentary silence, and, after a matter of minutes, the results which mercifully showed that no bones were broken but there was heavy bruising of her ribs. Her knee, too, was only cut and bruised.

She heard Alex's voice from what seemed a great distance and came out of her trance-like stupor.

'You've had a miraculous escape, thank God.'

'But it's damned painful,' said another voice, which belonged to Dr Mason.

Nicola looked around her and knew they were in a

small annexe next to the X-ray department. Her gaze went to Alex and then back to Dr Mason.

'If I can walk,' she said spiritedly, drawing on every scrap of courage and strength. The aching pain of her ribs made breathing and talking a supreme effort, for every movement was as if a burning knife had stabbed her in the chest. She made an attempt to get up, but her knee was stiff and she would have fallen had not Alex put his arm around her.

Dr Mason, a fair-haired youthful looking man of forty, with humorous blue eyes and a generous mouth, said, 'I think Dr Moncton will agree with me that you should stay here tonight. You've had a bad shaking.'

'Just,' Alex agreed, 'what the doctor ordered.' He held Nicola's gaze. 'And I'm serious.'

Woman-like, Nicola made a face. 'I've nothing *with* me. . .'

'I've already spoken to your mother,' Alex reassured her. 'She's bringing your things and should be here any minute.'

It was obvious he had already taken it upon himself to decide that she should stay overnight. She was very relieved that Jan was coming, and said so.

Dr Mason hurried away and a nurse appeared, saying by way of a cheerful greeting, 'I'm going to take you to your room, Nurse Hardy, and get you to bed. Dr Warner—the house physician—will give you a checkup. . . Your mother has arrived.'

Nicola murmured a smiling acknowledgement and expressed her pleasure at Jan's presence.

'You're Nurse Radleigh,' Alex said.

Nurse Radleigh, a fair-haired, pretty girl whose

excellent figure was outlined by the smart blue and white striped uniform, looked surprised. Doctors had not usually such good memories and she was flattered. She thought Alex was dishy and the most attractive among the visiting doctors.

'Yes.' She flashed him an understanding look. 'I was on your Mrs Whitby case.' She turned Nicola's chair towards the door.

Nicola said almost urgently to Alex, 'Thank you for all you've done.'

His voice was firm. 'I'll stay until you're settled.' Even as he spoke he wondered if to do so was wise, knowing that he must not take advantage of the circumstances to further his cause.

'I've spoilt your evening,' she murmured apologetically.

Their gaze met.

'The patient must always come first,' he said formally.

The remark distanced him and she saw only 'the doctor' doing his duty by his patient, the earlier familiarity gone.

Jan awaited Nicola when she was wheeled into a spacious room with its en suite bathroom, and avoided any undue fuss as she expressed her sympathy and concern. Only the bandaged knee bore obvious testimony to the fall, but Jan could appreciate the pain Nicola was enduring as, after the first greeting, she said, 'I bruised my ribs years ago, when they used to bind you up with Elastoplast. I was allergic to it and it brought me out in a terrific rash!'

'We don't bind even broken ribs today,' Nurse said, almost amused. She looked down at Nicola. 'Anything to do with ribs is painful,' she added sympathetically, the fact that Nicola was a nurse increasing her interest in the case.

Jan suffered with Nicola as Nurse manoeuvred her from her chair to the bed.

'Let me try to stand up,' Nicola said in a breath. She looked down at her swollen knee, which was expertly bandaged and would not bend.

'I couldn't get to the bathroom,' she said ruefully, viewing the prospect of the alternative bedpan with horror. But she swayed and was promptly helped into bed—a bed stacked with pillows to enable her to remain in a sitting position, her back entirely supported.

A few minutes later Jan left her, promising to return when Nicola had been assessed by Dr Warner. She felt helpless and bleak as she reached the corridor and was thankful to see Alex come out of a nearby room. They had previously exchanged a few words and she said, 'Nurse is getting Nicola settled...'

'Come with me,' he said, and put his hand against her elbow, guiding her to another passage and to a fair-sized room, comfortably furnished with easy chairs and a centre table on which stood a vase of dahlias and Michaelmas daises. The general colour scheme was deep pink and grey. 'This is where visitors and doctors meet...'

Jan sat down.

'How is she?' Her gaze was anxious and enquiring.

'In greater pain than the seriousness of her injuries,'

he said honestly. 'Nothing to worry about, but it will be a few weeks before the bruising subsides...it is a miracle that more damage was not done.'

Jan studied him, thankful for his presence and the fact that he had sought her help. There was no strangeness in his attitude and he might have been a relative. Looking at him, she was at a loss to understand why Nicola didn't realise that he was far more attractive than Stuart, and that a future with him would be full of possibilities.

'You've been so good,' she said gratefully. 'Prompt attention from one's doctor is the ultimate of luxury.'

He looked at Jan earnestly. 'It isn't difficult for me to take care of Nicola.' His voice was low and full of emotion. He added swiftly, 'But you know that, and my feelings generally.' It was a relief to unburden himself and he had a great affection for Jan, irrespective of the fact that she was Nicola's mother.

Jan felt that to dissemble would be an insult to his confidence. Her expression was sympathetic as she said gently, 'I have guessed.' She added honestly, 'But recently I've wondered if I wasn't wrong.'

Alex was completely open as he put her in the picture, ending with, 'So you see I can only respect her wishes and give her the space she desires.'

'Women don't always want to be taken at their word.'

He said instantly, 'So you think I'm wrong?'

'On the contrary. To be kept guessing will not do my daughter any harm. Seeming uninterest can be a challenge in circumstances like yours.'

Alex gave a half-smile. 'I was never a very good

actor, but I respect your views, and I take it I have your support?'

Jan met his dark intense gaze very directly. 'All the way; and I know that applies to Timothy also.'

A relieved smile spread over his features.

'You hearten me.'

Jan was grateful for his tenacity and the fact that his love for Nicola was deep enough to take her rebuffs in his stride. It was incredible to her that Nicola was unable to weigh up his worth against that of Stuart, who, even if he had been faithful, in no way measured up to Alex's standards or physical attraction.

Meanwhile Nicola had been prepared for the night, her gown replaced by a nightdress of silk and lace, which could easily be slipped from her shoulders. The effort and movement added to her pain and she felt faint and exhausted when, at last, she was able to pitch herself against the numerous pillows, the fragrance of her Guerlain talc removing the antiseptic smell that hung in the atmosphere. She took in the details of the room for the first time. It was medium-sized with a white chest of drawers, built-in cupboards and a useful locker beside her bed, on which her make-up mirror and necessities had been placed. Bright chintz curtains hung against apple-white walls, giving an atmosphere of friendliness and cutting out a deadening austerity. Two comfortable armchairs with matching chintz covers, and an upright chair and occasional table near the bed, completed the picture. The bathroom door was to the left and the entrance door faced her. A bed-table was across the foot of the bed.

Nurse Radleigh said with gentle satisfaction, 'You're

ready for Dr Warner now.' She added, 'We won't put your bed jacket on until he's been in...you're not cold?'

'The central heating's on?' Nicola made it seem a question.

'Oh, yes...'

'Why do I have to be seen by Dr Warner?' The words came wearily.

'As you know, all patients are seen on admission, to assess how they feel, or are, as a result of shock.' She gave Nicola a professional appraisal. 'You've been splendid.'

'And you have been so kind... Where did you train?'

'St Thomas's.'

'I was at the Middlesex...'

'You're the first nurse I've had here as a patient.' There was a warmth in the utterance.

'And this is the first time I've *been* a patient,' Nicola hastened, breathing with difficulty. 'Everything seems very different from this angle!' She winced and her face looked pinched. 'Do you live in Cheltenham? I mean——' Nicola didn't want to sound too inquisitive.

'I'm still at home...in Cheltenham.' Her face lit up. 'But I'm being married in the New Year.'

Nicola murmured her good wishes and depression seeped back.

'You've talked long enough,' Nurse Radleigh said after a second.

A knock came on the door.

'That will be Dr Warner.'

A moment later a tall slim young man entered,

announced himself and took his stethoscope from the pocket of his white coat as he reached the side of the bed. Nurse Radleigh moved a little way away and stood by the window.

'I hear you've been having an argument with some steps?'

Nicola liked the attitude of the man looking down at her. He conveyed sympathy with an understanding smile. He was dark, with a round boyish face and expressive blue eyes.

'My ribs objected,' Nicola said.

'Painful things, ribs,' he said quietly. 'Let's have a look at you.'

Nurse Radleigh came forward and adjusted Nicola's nightdress. In the next short while Nicola's heart, lungs and stomach, together with her blood-pressure, had been assessed. The thought flashed through Nicola's mind that Alex would have made this examination had she not stayed in hospital, and she felt a tremor at the possibility.

'You've certainly had a bashing!' he exclaimed ruefully, as he finished and her bed jacket was put on. 'You've been lucky not to have had any broken bones.' He held her gaze. 'You're feeling pretty battered.' There was sympathy in the utterance.

'I'm not going to pick a fight with anyone,' Nicola commented.

He laughed.

'I'll give you twenty milligrams of Temazepam and a couple of paracetamol. A good night's sleep is essential. . . You're familiar with all this, Nurse Hardy. I understand you're part of the Moncton practice.'

'Yes. . .at least I shall be able to get back to work quickly. A matter of grinning and bearing it since no bones are broken,' she said with a cheerfulness he admired.

'Something like that,' he agreed. 'Your knee will make walking awkward.'

Nicola nodded. 'One adjusts. And I shall thank heaven for my shower,' she murmured, willing herself to talk and not give way, as it would have been so easy to do.

Philip Warner looked at her with admiring approval. Life would be simple if all patients had her outlook and courage.

'I'll see you tomorrow morning,' he said as he prepared to leave.

'I shall be going home,' she said firmly.

'Which, for all your will-power, you are not fit to do this evening,' he said stoutly.

Nicola allowed herself to sink into the pain and not to fight it.

'I must admit,' she said a little wanly, 'that's true.'

'I hope you'll have a good night,' he said kindly.

When he had gone Nicola lay there in a pool of suffering, each breath painful. Where was Jan? And had Alex meant that he would see her when she was 'settled in'? There had been no reason, she thought, why he should stay, and yet she could not deny that she was glad he had intended to do so. 'The patient must always come first'. His words re-echoed, making her feel a little self-conscious and isolated.

Jan came in, gentle and sympathetic as she said, 'How now?'

'There's a word for it,' Nicola replied, 'but I'm so thankful I'm in one piece. I'd no idea that ribs could be so painful.' She wanted to ask about Alex and, as though sensing the fact, Jan said,

'I've been talking to Alex and have said goodbye to him.' She didn't make the mistake of praising him and wondered if Nicola might do so.

But all Nicola said was, 'It is a bonus to have your doctor as a friend at a time like this.' The words sounded practical and Jan merely nodded. The cool calculation didn't hearten her.

'I brought you your coat-dress,' Jan said, changing the subject. 'A nurse's uniform is not ideal as you are now. . .'

Nicola, weak and in pain, felt tears sting her eyes.

'You're so good,' she murmured. 'You thought of everything when you packed my case.' She put out a hand and clasped Jan's.

'I'm so thankful it isn't worse,' Jan said somewhat irrelevantly, but touched by Nicola's attitude. 'And now I'm going to leave you. I'll ring in the morning.'

'And come to fetch me,' Nicola said urgently.

'Of course. . . I've spoken to Timothy and he sends you his love.'

Nicola gave a little sigh of pleasure at the thought of him. She suddenly seemed a very lucky woman.

Nurse Radleigh came in as Jan left.

'Something to eat,' she suggested, and studied Nicola intently.

Nicola said immediately, 'Nothing, thank you.'

'Ovaltine?'

'Yes, please.'

'You're to be settled in for the night.'

Nicola noticed that the travelling-clock Jan had brought said nine. It seemed an eternity. But the thought of sleep and escape from pain offered a glimpse of heaven.

'I won't object,' she promised.

As Nurse Radleigh reached the door on her way out, Alex stood there.

'Ah! Doctor.'

'Can I see your patient?'

'Most certainly, and I am then going to give her some Ovaltine and tablets.'

The door closed. Alex moved towards the bed.

She looked up at him and felt shy. What was he thinking?

He lifted the high-backed chair and sat down beside her.

'I've spoken to Dr Warner and he is satisfied with your general condition. It will take time for the bruising to subside. Unfortunately we cannot accelerate the process. . . Have they made you as comfortable as possible?' He indicated the pillows.

'Oh, yes.' She spoke with appreciation. 'And Dr Warner was very kind.'

Alex studied her intently, noticing the attractive bed jacket and the moulding of her breasts beneath it, reminding himself at the same time that he was her doctor. Nevertheless, he longed to put his arms around her and end the pretence.

There was a tension between them as she said firmly, 'I want to get back to work as soon as possible.'

He warned her, 'I shall be the judge of that.'

DOCTOR'S TEMPTATION 157

It struck her that he was very much 'the doctor' as he sat there, just as he had been after the X-rays. For a moment, loneliness overcame her as though pain had sensitised her and awakened emotions that had lain dormant for so long, making her crave the sympathy and tenderness he had betrayed at the moment of, and after, her fall. A gulf seemed to have widened between them as his gaze met hers with professional assessment; and, while she did not deceive herself about her feelings, she knew she wanted him to kiss her, hold her; desire heightened by weakness as she looked into his dark, inscrutable eyes.

CHAPTER NINE

NICOLA, embarrassed, dismissed her momentary lapse and shut her mind against emotions aroused wholly by circumstances and physical weakness. She was, she told herself critically, like a child craving a teddy bear to cuddle, and the idea disgusted her. Irrationally, she wanted Alex to leave; his presence disconcerted her, emphasising the fact that there was no one in her life, with the exception of her parents, to whom she was close; no one to whom she mattered outside the bond of friendship. And, while she had deliberately chosen that unemotional wilderness, it now seemed a rather frighteningly lonely place.

'You've not had anything to eat,' she said abruptly, relieving the tension.

He glanced at his watch.

'I've to give Mrs Ross her injection after I've looked in on Mr Black.' Both patients were terminal cancer cases.

Nicola nodded solemnly, but persisted with concern, 'You must eat.'

He got to his feet.

'It is for the doctor to worry about the patient,' he suggested, 'not for her to worry about him; but thank you for the thought. . . Goodnight, Nicola.' His deep voice enhanced the sound of her name.

She watched him move to the door.

'Thank you again for all you've done. Jan will fetch me in the morning.' There was a trace of firmness in her shaky voice.

'Dr Warner will see you first.'

'He couldn't *prevent* my leaving.'

'He could advise against it.'

'And you?' She added with all the strength she could muster, 'You're my doctor.'

'I'm not in charge of your case here. . .let's leave it until the morning and see how you are.' He had reached the door and his hand was on the knob. 'I'll be in touch.'

Did that mean in touch with *her*, or with Dr Warner? she asked herself.

He left, and immediately Nurse Radleigh came in with the Ovaltine and medication. Nicola sighed. Depression seeped into her like fog and not all her self-criticism and analysis dispersed it. A little later, she drifted mercifully to sleep.

Meanwhile Alex attended to his patients and returned home, telling his father all that had transpired since he put him in the picture at the time of the fall. Philip was aware of the strain in Alex's voice and manner, and said reassuringly, 'Only a matter of time . . .you'll miss her.'

Alex was immediately alert and betrayed the trend of his thoughts without realising it.

'She's not going away or——'

Philip interjected, 'I meant in the practice.'

There was a moment of significant silence.

Alex, aware of his father's scrutiny, said dismissively, 'Of course.' His feelings were too near the surface for him to want to discuss Nicola. He had hated leaving her on such an unemotional note and knew that the task he had set himself would become more of an ordeal than ever as a result of her accident. His thoughts became chaotic: suppose he was adopting the wrong attitude by humouring her, even though Jan agreed with him?

'A brandy would not be amiss,' Philip said deliberately. 'I'll join you and, oh—Mrs Beckett left you some sandwiches in the dining-room.'

Alex welcomed the idea of the brandy, which Philip poured. He didn't want the sandwiches that the housekeeper had prepared, but sat down in the comfortable sitting-room of his father's flat and thrust his legs out in front of him wearily.

'I lost Mrs Ross,' he said with a sigh.

Philip felt a pang. He knew that Mrs Ross was in her early fifties. His own bereavement was never far away. He looked at Alex. Words weren't necessary.

Nicola, Alex thought a few seconds later, would be asleep and out of pain. He had wanted so desperately to comfort her, to take his place at her side. It wouldn't be easy to continue to play the doctor, their previous arguments and disagreements giving way to pleasant formality and careful concern, as in the beginning. He looked around the room, taking in the Chippendale cabinet, deep armchairs and general air of comfort—an air which his mother's art in furnishing had always created—and visualised a situation in which he and Nicola would create a home. . . He wished he could fetch her from the nursing home should she be ready to leave tomorrow. He could arrange his work accordingly and Allan would help, to say nothing of his father. But

Nicola would not wish that, because it would establish a close relationship, which was the last thing she wanted. His seeing her into the nursing home was a different matter. An accident and an emergency made their own rules and he felt, with some degree of satisfaction, that she had been glad of his support.

The two men sat and talked fitfully and in harmony. Philip was not decieved and knew that Alex was in love with Nicola, unable to assess her feelings, while aware of her unhappiness and discontent. Both had lived through traumatic experiences and he could only hope that Nicola would eventually emulate Alex and rise above it. It also struck him that Alex was just the type of man Nicola needed, to curb her wilfulness and bring out all the sterling qualities he felt sure she possessed.

Nicola awakened the following morning and a general stiffness was added to the bruising. It took her a few minutes to assess the situation and recall the events of the previous evening, and even as she reflected on her position and the intense aching of her body she was aware of the activity of the nursing home and the echo of footsteps. Nurse Radleigh appeared with a cup of tea.

'You've had a good night,' she said brightly. 'I'm just going off duty. . .how are you feeling?'

Nicola bore the discomfort with fortitude.

'Battered, but better in myself.' Her thoughts clicked back to her own nursing days and the routine that was part of it. Under ordinary hospital rules, Nurse Radleigh would have written up her chart of pulse, respiration and temperature, and got her washed or bathed ready for the day staff to take over.

As if reading her mind, Nurse Radleigh hastened, 'An auxiliary nurse will come and make you comfortable. We bend the rules here and you can decide what you want for breakfast.'

Nicola realised she had not eaten since the previous lunchtime, and then only had a sandwich. Now she was empty but not hungry. The thought of Alex floated over the conversation.

'Dr Moncton rang; and your mother. Your mother will ring back later.' She indicated the telephone by the bed. 'I gave her your room number.'

Nicola sipped the tea. 'Thank you.'

A new nurse appeared in the doorway. She wore a deep blue uniform, was well-built, with natural colour and bright observant eyes. Nurse Radleigh said cheerfully, 'This is Nurse Wilton, who will look after you.' She left them, appreciating Nicola's warm thanks.

'If,' Nicola said swiftly, 'I could get to the bathroom. . .' She added urgently, '*Please*——'

Nurse Wilton smiled.

'There are no instructions that you must not get out of bed,' she said reassuringly. 'Being a nurse yourself, you will know that bedpans and false teeth are the two bugbears for patients!'

Nicola leant heavily on Nurse Wilton as she made her way to the bathroom. Her ribs felt torn and she limped painfully, but the task was accomplished. By the time Nicola returned to bed she realised that only willpower and determination were going to enable her to go home that day. Breathing was an effort and every movement jarred.

'It's quite ridiculous that a few bruises can be such a nuisance,' she said disgustedly. 'My knee is straightforward pain and you can deal with that; it doesn't affect your breathing——'

Nurse Wilton said stoutly, 'You've done very well, and the paracetamol will help.'

Nicola overcame the spasm of faintness and knew she could not face up to breakfast.

'Just a cup of coffee, please,' she said, and felt that Alex was chiding her. She could almost hear him saying, 'You will not help yourself by going without food.' Her thoughts raced. Would she be able to manage to get into the car? Why was it so urgent to get home? Obviously because she would have her parents to look after her, and if she needed a doctor Alex would be available. He would get his visiting nurse to dress her knee. . .whereas here. . . She didn't know why it seemed such a wilderness when it was the height of comfort and efficiency.

Domestic staff brought her coffee and Nurse Wilton said with a touch of authority, 'I ordered scrambled egg, which, when put in front of you. . .' She paused hopefully as the appetisingly laid tray was placed on the bed table and slid into position.

Nicola's stomach didn't revolt at the sight of food. She noticed appreciatively the china coffee-pot and cup and saucer. The Cotswold Nursing Home had not won its excellent reputation for nothing. She was glad Alex had brought her there. Had he left a message? Nurse Radleigh didn't say, and would assume that she, Nicola, would accept the fact that it was merely an enquiry to know how she was. He most certainly wouldn't send his love, and, once told that she was all right, would have no reason to ring back. By the time she had allowed her thoughts to ramble over that issue she had almost eaten the scrambled egg without realising it.

The telephone rang a little later and she gave a gasp of pain as she immediately reached out and lifted the receiver.

'Jan. . .no, I haven't seen Dr Warner yet. *Alex* been in touch?' Nicola hastened, 'Why?'

Jan spoke in a matter-of-fact voice, but was aware that Nicola had tensed and that her voice was querulous. 'He wondered if his car would be better for you to get into should you come home today—or whenever you come home. Ours hasn't the same leg room as his Volvo, and it served you well last evening.'

Why, she asked herself, should Alex ask Jan that and not *her*? She knew, however, that he had a valid point.

'I can't arrange anything until I've seen Dr Warner.' Nicola was precise.

'Obviously,' Jan replied, 'Alex realised that, and it was left that he'd ring me later when a decision had been made. It is up to you.'

'Alex can't drop everything to ferry me about,' Nicola suggested. 'And I hate not knowing when I can leave.'

Jan said with a little laugh, 'Don't be difficult, darling. You can cope with the Volvo. Neither my car, nor Timothy's, is as spacious.'

Nicola didn't know why she felt in a difficult mood.

'I could arrange for an ambulance,' she suggested pertly.

Jan felt irritated.

'That would hardly be gracious, with a perfectly good car at your disposal. Obviously the nursing home could provide you with any transport you required, but. . .' She paused before adding, 'What shall I tell Alex?'

A flush rose in Nicola's face as she recalled her reaction to him the previous evening. His name suddenly had significance.

'Thank him and tell him I'd be grateful,' she said, adding swiftly, 'Ask him to ring me.' The words came out spontaneously. 'He has enquired this morning, but I wasn't disturbed.'

Jan already knew that from Alex, and it was left that she would pass on Nicola's message.

Dr Warner gave Nicola permission to go home.

'I don't need to tell you take things easily,' he said with a rueful smile. 'Your limitations will be only too evident. Dr Moncton will arrange for your knee to be dressed.' He left with an air of friendliness.

Alex rang a little later. Nicola had been waiting anxiously for his call, while pretending to read a newspaper.

It struck her that he had a particularly attractive telephone voice, but that his inflexion was purely matter-of-fact. He was glad she was able to go home and he would easily come to fetch her. It would be about three.

'I don't want to put you out,' she insisted.

'You won't. Everything's under control. I'm glad you

feel strong enough to make the effort.' His voice was smooth. 'See you at three,' he added briskly. The line went dead.

Nicola stared down at the receiver as she replaced it. There was a sense of dissatisfaction as she reflected on the call. It had been kindly, but impersonal. She frowned. Wasn't that what she wanted? He was showing her every consideration and in that moment she could not help comparing him with Stuart, to Stuart's detriment. Stuart had been a selfish type when it came to it. No pang touched her as she faced up to reality, and a strange unease possessed her. It didn't seem possible that she was criticising Stuart quite apart from condemnation, or that she could contemplate him so calmly. She avoided facing up to the fact that the wound had healed and she was faced with the truth. Her pulse quickened as she reflected on her behaviour during the past months and her attitude towards Alex. He had been so good to her, endeavoured to help her in every way, their similar experiences and initial unhappiness creating a bond which she had done her best to denigrate. She felt suddenly that she must redeem herself in his eyes; even confide in him her new emotional reaction to the past. A little bubble of happiness touched her for the first time since her engagement was broken: the bruising and discomfort even seemed more bearable. Just as three o'clock seemed years away.

Stoically and with supreme efort she managed to struggle into her underwear and coat-dress with Nurse Wilton's help. The result was attractive and smart. The coat-dress, two shades of blue, made her pencil-slim.

She looked pale and wide-eyed. Bruises had come out on her forearms, now covered, and every step she took was a painful effort. She sat down carefully on the bed. It was five to three. A soft sapphire cashmere coat lay beside her.

'I'll wait until Dr Moncton comes before I put that on,' she said.

Nurse Wilton laughed.

'You may have a long wait.' Inwardly she told herself that she wouldn't mind being bruised if the palliative was to have Dr Moncton fetching her!

But Alex was punctual. He came into the room with an almost businesslike air, made reference to the fact that she was dressed and included Nurse Wilton in the conversation. Then, 'And how is your patient?' he asked.

It wasn't the atmosphere Nicola wanted and she said critically, 'Why do doctors and nurses always talk together as though the patient weren't there?' She added, 'I'm quite capable of telling you how I am.'

She saw the look of near astonishment flash into Alex's face. His voice humoured her: he might have been speaking to a child.

'And how *are* you?' He held her gaze disconcertingly.

She felt foolish and ungracious.

'I hurt all over,' she admitted honestly, aware of his smart dark suit and forceful personality, which dominated the scene. Then, not wanting to complain, added, 'I've had a lucky escape.' Her mood changed. 'I've everything to be grateful for.'

Alex wanted both to shake her and take her in his arms, knowing that she would like to be difficult and unable to fathom exactly why. Her vulnerability disarmed him and put him at the mercy of his emotions, and he knew that the part he would be called upon to play during the next week or so would be both demanding and dangerous. Because he had decided on a line of action didn't mean it would be easy to follow.

'If you're ready,' he said with a gentle patience.

Nurse Wilton helped Nicola into her coat—a difficult task.

'It's cold out!' Alex exclaimed. 'A crisp October day. . .'

'It's beautifully warm in here. . . I can do a good line in a limp-shuffle,' she added with a smile, not wanting to make a fuss as she got to her feet.

But Alex said immediately, 'A porter is coming with a chair.'

Nicola remembered that they were on the second floor and had come up in the lift.

'A stick will be essential when you get home,' Nurse Wilton said practically.

Nicola gave a little laugh.

'The dear old lady!'

In a few minutes the porter had arrived and Nicola was eased into the chair. She shook hands with Nurse Wilton, who said, 'Thank you for being such a good patient.'

Nicola looked back into the room. A great deal seemed to have happened to her while she was there, and as she glanced up at Alex emotion stirred. He was so calm, so very much in control and, above all, the doctor.

Life seemed very strange when viewed from a wheelchair. The corridor to the lift telescoped, and the patients and nurses seemed particularly tall as they passed her by, each glancing in her direction, some with a smile. The sensation in the lift as it went down seemed to stop her heart beating for an instant and she realised how weak she felt—almost faint.

'All right?' Alex's voice was that of questioning concern. He stood beside the chair as though on guard. She would have liked to hold his hand, and chided herself for the impulse.

'Yes,' she assured him.

A second or two later they reached the busy reception hall. Sister Adams—on duty because of the illness of a colleague and having only had a few hours' rest—came forward.

'Leaving us so soon, Nurse Hardy. . . Oh, we know that our patients are grateful to be admitted, but delighted to be let out. I don't have to ask how you are! Your bruising will not have vanished overnight.' She looked from Nicola to Alex, 'You're still in good hands. . . Yes, Nurse——' as an apologetic nurse approached her, obviously with a problem, and she hurried away, saying goodbye as she went.

Alex had brought the car right up to the wide doors used by the ambulance and stretcher cases. He and a porter manipulated Nicola into it and she sank painfully, but gratefully, into the comfortable seat. She rested against him a little longer than was necessary, conscious of his nearness. For a second their eyes met, his guarded, hers questioning, and as she drew back from him she realised with sudden overwhelming desire that she was in love with him.

Nicola was conscious only of Alex's presence beside her on the short journey home. She told herself that she was mad, dreaming, and that she could not have transferred her affections from Stuart to him after all she had suffered at Stuart's hands. Thoughts chased each other through her mind, uppermost the realisation of the strength and compassion in Alex as compared with the selfishness of Stuart.

'Those are very deep thoughts,' Alex said after a lengthy silence.

She felt suddenly shy and ill-at-ease, unable to assess his feelings and aware of her own irrational behaviour, even ungraciousness, during the past weeks. A little flame of anger sprang to life as she studied his attractive profile: what was he thinking? What *did* he think of her and how could she let him know how *she* felt? Colour rose in her cheeks as she knew he was waiting for some comment on his remark and she said falteringly, 'One is very vulnerable at times like these.'

Alex judged instantly that she was thinking of Stuart and said almost coldly, 'And often sees things out of perspective.'

She flashed back, 'Or has the truth forced upon one.' She gave a little gasp of pain. 'Sorry,' she hastened, 'it doesn't do to get worked up when one's ribs are like mine.'

Alex was confounded by her attitude. It was like dealing with quicksilver and he despaired of ever finding her in a compromising mood.

'Getting worked up is not what the doctor ordered,' he warned her.

She thought unreasonably, why couldn't he *see* that she loved him?

'And you are very much the doctor,' she challenged. Her thoughts swirled back. Once he had kissed her with compassion; now he seemed remote and professional. It wasn't so much what he *said* as his attitude.

His voice was almost stern. 'That is my role in your life.'

She groaned inwardly. And she had been the one to insist that she didn't want to be regarded with him as a pair. How strictly he was adhering to her edict and yet—the thought comforted her—how tenderly he had treated her the previous evening when she had needed him most. Another thought stabbed: that was all in the course of duty.

'That is my role in your life.'

She wished she could shout out that she didn't want it to be. It disturbed her that he had never before made his position so plain.

'I thought we were friends,' she blurted out shakily.

'The two are not imcompatible,' he suggested calmly. 'The doctor-patient relationship comes into a special category. Its limitations,' he added deliberately, 'are obvious.'

Uncomfortable though she was, Nicola didn't want the journey to end, although nothing he said offered her any hope. He had made their position very plain and her heart was heavy. She felt that she was standing at the bottom of a very steep hill which was impossible to climb.

A few desultory remarks were made during the rest of the journey and, almost in panic as they neared home, she asked, 'Are you very busy for the rest of the day?' She gave a little nervous laugh. 'And that's a silly question, because you're always busy. . .has this put you out very much?'

Her interest and conciliatory attitude did not go unnoticed by him. She seemed to have changed even since leaving the nursing home.

'I rearranged one or two appointments,' he answered conversationally. 'No question of my being put out. . . And now you're home.'

It seemed years since last she had been there. Her thoughts swirled. She was in love with Alex and could find no answering spark within him. Panic assailed her at the prospect of his leaving her.

His nearness was a torment as he manoeuvred her into the flat. She wanted to cry out, to tell him how she felt, while he, in turn, longed to kiss her into submission, yet determined to stay the course he had set himself in the hope of winning her love. He noticed with a tingling sensation of satisfaction how she pressed against him as he got her into the flat with Jan's help, but did not build up the fact because of the circumstances.

'I feel ninety!' Nicola gasped as she reached the sofa. 'One takes mobility for granted.' She stood for a second, her arm through Alex's. Once she let go, the last physical contact with him would vanish. He looked at her guardedly, the tension unbearable. Then, almost abruptly, he eased her down amid the cushions, the task completed as she lay back, exhausted.

'Thank you,' she murmured, lifting her legs and

getting them into a comfortable position. 'I'm not going to lie about,' she added somewhat aggressively.

Alex held her gaze. 'For once you will do as you are told,' he said half banteringly. '"Lying about", as you call it, is not the answer, but care until the bruising has subsided a little is necessary. Not that I'm a bit afraid you'll want to start hoovering!'

'I want to get back to work.' She looked up at him, her heart thumping as she was conscious of his attractiveness. Emotion overwhelmed her. She added, 'How will you manage?'

His voice was matter-of-fact.

'Mrs Latimer has arranged for a friend of hers to come in. She had just left her job at Cheltenham General.'

Nicola felt a stab of jealousy and exclaimed, 'Proving that no one is indispensable!'

Would he contradict her? Would he say something reassuring?

But he made no comment and Jan hastened, 'It's early, but would you like a cup of tea?' She had remained silent while Nicola was being attended to.

Alex didn't hesitate. 'Afraid I haven't time.'

Nicola sensed that there was a rapport between her mother and Alex which seemed significant and isolated her, Nicola, in some way. She could not take her gaze away from Alex, and noticed every expression on his face, every intonation of his voice, which gave meaning to all his remarks. When would she see him again? The prospect of his absence turned her world into a wilderness.

Alex nerved himself to meet Nicola's eyes and said

easily, 'I'll look in tomorrow, and if you're in any trouble give me a ring.' He turned to Jan as he added, 'I'll arrange for Nurse Bennet to come in and dress the knee in the morning.'

Nicola watched him walk towards the door and when he turned she said, 'Thank you; and thank you for yesterday.' She ached to have his arms around her and despaired at his going.

His smile was an answer.

Jan went to his side and walked with him to the front door. She told herself that his manner would intrigue any woman, and inwardly congratulated him upon it.

'We're very grateful, Alex,' she said appreciatively.

He looked down at her; words were unnecessary.

When Jan returned to Nicola there was an empty silence for a minute. All that had ever been said about Alex seemed to lie between them.

Nicola murmured half apologetically, 'He's been very kind.'

Jan nodded. 'Alex is a man who would always be there when he was needed. . . I'm glad he's got a nurse to take your place.' Jan was aware that the words were very direct.

Nicola's voice boomed as much as the bruising would allow, 'It won't be for long.' She looked at Jan and then quickly dropped her gaze. 'I'll try not to be like the proverbial bear with the sore head while I'm at home, but inactivity is not my idea of heaven.'

Jan was studying Nicola intently, aware of some subtle change in her that she could not fathom.

'I didn't realise you were so absorbed in your present job?' The words came tentatively.

Nicola replied tensely, 'We are a good team.'

'Julie being there——' Jan broke off. 'I like Barry.' She spoke disjointedly. 'They make a good pair.'

Nicola winced. The words stung. Her words to Alex came back mockingly. Could she expect any man to take that rebuff and ever pursue her again, even had he the desire to do so? She went over the events of the previous evening and tears stung her eyes as she faced the fact that everything Alex had done for her had been in line with his careful kindness and compassion. At no time had he conveyed the idea of a man attracted sexually to a woman. A man falling in love. As he said, his role in her life was that of a doctor and a friend. Her heart ached and desire flamed. How was it possible in such circumstances to win his love?

CHAPTER TEN

It was two weeks later when October had given way to a cold foggy November that Alex, having examined Nicola's knee, said, 'You won't be needing my services any longer. You've been very lucky and the healing process has been excellent.'

She looked down at him as he sat on the stool at her feet, watching him get up and replace the stool by the side of her chair. She was conscious of him to the exclusion even of what he was saying, feeling the power of his personality and his dominance over her to a point where only love and desire had any meaning. His manner had not changed during those weeks and her frustration had increased. Her heart seemed to be beating in a hollow body as she said, 'That means I can return to work.' She watched him carefully as she spoke and he stood before her, obviously not intending to sit down and stay for a while. It was six-thirty and she wondered what he was doing that evening.

'Most certainly, if you wish,' he said easily.

She immediately rose to that.

'Meaning that you are satisfied to keep your present nurse?'

Alex had come no nearer to understanding her and he found it almost impossible to gauge her feelings. There had been occasions when she had been amenable and he had felt that he was making progress, only for the old aggression to manifest itself when least expected.

He said with a cool patience, 'Meaning nothing of the kind. . . I merely wondered if you'd like a little time to get around more; even have a weekend off to stay with old friends.'

Obviously, she thought with a desperate rebellion, he was not depending on her presence in any way.

'That's the last thing,' she retorted. 'They're all far too busy with their own affairs, anyway.'

He looked at her and said deliberately, 'Which is perfectly normal.'

Instantly she came back with, 'Meaning that I am not?' If only she could master the emotion that swept over her at the sight of him. He looked so powerful as he stood there, and she wanted his arms around her, and the ecstasy of knowing that he loved her. *Loved her*. The words mocked her. She was just someone he had helped through a bad experience, and whose ideas clashed with his own. The friendly doctor, as he had made it quite plain. The fact tormented her.

Alex said carefully, 'You have made your own rules, Nicola. Because I respect them doesn't mean that I have to agree with them.' He held her gaze disarmingly, 'One day you will have to begin to live again.' He hastened before she had time to make a telling reply, 'I must be going. I'm due at a dinner party at eight and have a patient to see beforehand.'

Nicola felt a hollow misery. Now he didn't even tell her whose dinner party it was! Once she would have been going with him. What a *fool* she'd been. Her own helplessness tormented her. She wanted to shriek her frustration. And he had shown no enthusiasm for her return to work, either!

'I've taken up your time,' she said evasively, wanting to be reassured. His words, 'One day you will have to begin to live again,' struck an ironic note, for *life*, as represented by him, was only a few steps from her.

He looked at her disarmingly.

'Not at all,' he commented casually. He added easily, 'I think it would be a good idea if you returned to work on Monday week. It's Friday now,' he reflected. 'I don't want to dismiss Nurse Hamlin——'

Nicola cursed herself for betraying her chagrin. 'Would it be easier if she stayed on?' The words rapped out.

His gaze was masterfully critical.

'Do you enjoy taking everything I say the wrong way?'

She felt his anger and irritation, and a sick sensation of depression settled upon her. 'It isn't a question of that,' she murmured.

'Then what is it?' he demanded.

Now she couldn't bear to be out of harmony with him. It struck deep and painfully.

He was aware that she looked dismayed and reflected that at least he had the power to rouse her to annoyance: he dared not take it as far as jealousy.

She said boldly, 'That you might like Nurse Hamlin to stay on.'

His voice was harsh. 'When I no longer need your services I shall tell you. You have a positive genius for misunderstanding me. It so happens that Nurse Hamlin has retired, but likes working from time to time and is a very good link to have in an emergency, as we have proved.'

Nicola felt small.

He stared at her in amazement as she said contritely, 'I'm sorry.' Her voice broke.

Emotion lay just beneath the surface as their eyes met. She thought of his kiss and, now, of her longing to have his lips on hers.

He mastered desire with a superhuman effort and said, 'Then we'll make it Monday week; use those days to enjoy yourself as much as you can.'

She couldn't think of anything to say. Her pulse was racing and she dreaded the moment when he would leave her.

'I must be going,' he said abruptly. And, hating the words, added, 'Until Monday week.'

With that he saw himself out as usual. She remained inert: he had taken her world with him. How coolly he accepted the fact that he would not see her until Monday week, and how obvious it was that the time factor was of no importance. She sat there feeling helpless and defeated.

Nicola returned to work with a determination to make Alex aware of her as a woman who was part of his life and profession, and to endear herself in a wholly different way from the past with its arguments and irritations.

The staff welcomed her back and Julie said warmly, 'Now we're a team again. It has seemed all wrong without you.'

Nicola was dying to ask if Alex had expressed any

sense of loss at her absence, but could not bring herself to do so.

Betty Latimer studied Nicola as she added her welcome to Julie's, and thought there was something different about her: that she seemed softer and less aggressive, which on the face of it was ridiculous unless physical suffering had dulled a former disillusionment, and made her see life in better perspective.

Nicola was waiting for Alex to appear, hoping she might see him before she went into her room and dealt with the first patient; she even toyed with the possibility that he might be early in order to welcome her back, and then blushed at her own conceit. She had nothing on which to base her hopes, not even a telephone call during those nine days which had been an eternity to her.

And suddenly he appeared at the door of her room, making her heart miss a beat at the sight of him.

'Welcome back.' His deep voice thrilled her.

She tried to tell herself that there was an intimacy in his smile, but knew she was imagining it and that his expression was merely friendly.

'It's good to *be* back,' she said and lowered her gaze after meeting his.

'You're looking well. . .we've a pretty hectic day.'

He noticed how beautiful she was as she sat there at her desk, and thought how much he had missed her, longing to pick up the telephone and invite her to dinner. . . Was there any change in her? Had she missed him? At least she had said it was good to be back. And she had *come* back. He was haunted by the fear that she might decide to return to hospital life, finding the memories of Cheltenham unbearable.

Nicola fought against the emotion that surged over her, but kept her voice light as she said, 'We shall survive!'

Stupid words, she told herself, but she could not think of any others.

He accepted that as phlegmatic and as a note on which to leave.

'Yes,' he echoed, 'we shall survive.' And with that he hurried away.

Nicola clenched her hands. Couldn't she have managed to say something more personal, or more intimate? His presence remained, as though he had stamped his personality on the room merely by standing in the doorway. And again she felt his arms around her as he helped her that fateful night. . .

'Hi!'

Nicola heard Julie's voice as from a great distance, and jerked herself to attention.

'You were miles away. . . Mrs Sinclair wonders if you can fit her in.'

The name sounded foreign until Nicola remembered that she was the patient who'd had a bad fall weeks before.

'I certainly will. . . A fellow feeling!' Nicola added.

Allan came in at that moment. He and Rosie had been mystified about Nicola during the past weeks, and the easy familiarity had vanished, but, as she greeted him, he thought that her voice was softer and more welcoming.

'I've missed you all,' she said unexpectedly in greeting.

He smiled. 'Praise indeed; we can return the compliment.' He added deliberately, 'We must get together and celebrate.' He watched her carefully, remembering the times they had been rebuffed.

'I'd like that.' Nicola recalled Alex's words, 'One day you'll have to begin to live again.' 'Give my love to Rosie.'

Allan looked pleased. He was at a loss to understand why Nicola's attitude had changed, but delighted that it had done so. He went out with a cheery, 'See you later.'

Nicola concentrated on her job, sliding back into the old routine with enthusiasm; but at the back of her mind was the image and thought of Alex. Would he look in again? Would she see him before she left that day? Or even at lunchtime? She found herself subconsciously listening for the sound of his voice and working herself up into a nervous state when he could be heard in the vicinity of the offices.

After lunch she made a valid excuse to see him in his consulting-room, having got Julie to make the arrangement.

'Well? How's it going?' he asked considerately.

If only, she thought fiercely, he weren't so attractive and authoritative; if only she could look at him with calm indifference instead of near fury because his treatment of her was kind, smooth and wholly friendly. It was impossible to know what he was really thinking. Yet why should he be thinking anything? He had simply taken her at her word. Rebellion built up as emotion flared.

'I think,' she said with concern, 'that you should see Mrs Trent.'

His eyes widened. He indicated the patients' chair and, as she sat down, took his place at his desk, looking at her in some surprise.

'Are you making an assessment, or giving me advice?' The words were measured.

'Both,' she said, letting emotion betray itself in her voice. 'Mrs Trent has vertigo and——'

His voice was quietly patient. 'I know Mrs Trent's complaint. She has her Stemetil and——'

'She isn't well and has bad heads, but doesn't want to *trouble* you. If you'd *see* her. . .'

Alex stared at Nicola in amazement. What mood had she to be in to make suggestions about his treatment of his patients? He got to his feet with a kind of restless indignation as he said, 'I'm available to all my patients, but if they don't ask to see me I'm not a mind-reader. Mrs Trent has all the distressing symptoms of vertigo—the giddiness being the worst——' He spread his hands out helplessly. 'What *is* all this?' He looked anxious. 'You've probably come back too soon and are seeing things out of proportion——'

In that moment Nicola felt emotion—longing, desire—flood over her until she lost all control as she cried, 'I'm not seeing things out of proportion; it is you who are blind——'

There was a second of tense, unbearable silence before he rapped out, '*Blind*? What do you mean?'

She had gone too far to stop as she caught at her

breath and the words tumbled out. 'I mean that I'm tired of your careful consideration. I want more than that——' Her voice rose until she almost yelled, 'Can't you see that I'm in love with you; that I can't stand our present relationship——?'

He stared at her aghast and disbelieving; then, holding her gaze in a masterful challenge, he reached her side and almost lifted her from her chair, gripping her arms as he demanded in bewilderment, 'Say that again——'

She shivered at his touch, her voice strong. 'I love you. . .' And in that second she realised the enormity of what she had done. 'And now I've no pride left. . . you must despise me as——'

But his lips stifled her last words, as they parted hers in a deep passionate kiss that drew from her every scrap of emotion, and left them vulnerable and at the mercy of the ecstasy of desire as they clung together, body against body, as though nothing could ever tear them apart, until finally, exhausted, he drew back and cried, 'Oh, my darling; if you knew how much I love you. . .!'

Nicola's heartbeat was choking her as she gasped, 'I can't believe it. . . I've wanted to be like this, here, in your arms, but I never thought——' She buried her face against his shoulder in confusion, as he tightened his grip. After a second she looked up at him wonderingly. 'You *love* me. . . Oh, Alex; what a fool I've been!'

The intercom went, making them jump, almost like a fire alarm. They were dragged back to reality and the fact that they were on duty and had work to do. Alex made a gesture of despair as he spoke to Julie...yes, he would see the next patient.

Nicola, almost shyly, said, 'Will you come to supper this evening? There's so *much*——' She stopped, almost in embarrassment, and moved to the door. This was Alex to whom she was speaking and the thrill of the intimacy silenced her.

'At seven,' he said forcefully, reaching her side. 'I've *got* to carry on now,' he added with a desperate sigh of regret.

Nicola looked up at him, her eyes starry. His kiss was deep and penetrating, and they clung together before she left with the parting words, 'Until seven.'

His voice was a low whisper. 'Yes, my darling.'

'*My darling*'. She might never have heard those words before, she thought, and hurried away as the patient appeared.

Jan took one look at Nicola as she rushed into the flat that evening, and gave a visible gasp.

Nicola didn't hesitate. 'Alex loves me,' she said with an almost wild happiness. She put her arms around her mother and waltzed her about the room, stopping before Jan had time to speak. 'Have you any smoked salmon? He's coming to supper and we don't want a proper meal!'

Jan's heart seemed to lift a few inches.

'I'm so glad... Yes, I have some smoked salmon.' Jan looked bewildered; she had not expected developments so soon, or even hoped for them.

'I've been a fool and a pain in the neck,' Nicola admitted. 'Will you forgive me if I talk later?' She

looked at Jan with deep love. 'You and Timothy have
been wonderful. You both deserve medals as big as
frying-pans. . . Did you hear that?' she asked as
Timothy came into the room.

'Very reassuring!' he exclaimed with a grin. He took
one look at her. 'Come into a fortune?'

Nicola kissed them both in a beguiling 'thank you'
fashion.

'Jan will tell you,' she said and dashed out of the
room, raiding the fridge before going to her own rooms.

Alex was coming to supper. *Alex loved her*. And
there was still so much for them to say. Was it real, or
was she having some enchanted dream? Her heart sang;
the hush of the November evening, with the table lamps
glowing in the sitting-room, offered a perfect sanctuary
for lovers. . .'Please God, don't let him be called out,'
she murmured to herself as she showered after making
the open smoked salmon sandwiches and putting out
the champagne glasses. Timothy had given her the
champagne some time previously, and she had put it in
the fridge the moment she got in.

By six-forty she was all ready, looking radiant in a
soft petunia-shaded cashmere skirt and matching top
with a jade motif on one shoulder. Another twenty
minutes. . . Jan would let him in and he would come
through to her on his own. She didn't want any gathering until she and Alex had spent the evening together.
She fingered the glasses on the silver tray; moved plates
and napkins almost blindly; sat down, and looked at
the clock. . . She was waiting for *Alex*; Alex, her doctor
whom she had first met when she had flu. A thrill went
over her. . .and then her cheeks burned. She had told

him that she loved him. . . How *could* she. . .? That was the front doorbell. . .

And, suddenly, it seemed the most natural thing in the world that he should be standing before her, there, in her own room. *Dr Alex*, looking at her with a passionate desire and yet a strange tenderness.

'It was worth being interrupted by my patient this afternoon, for us to have this moment,' he said as he took her in his arms and looked deep into her eyes before his mouth crushed hers, ecstasy like a flame between them. He said hoarsely, 'You were quite right; I've been blind and stupid. I should have told you I love you. . . I was afraid to do so that day when I kissed you. God knows I wanted to!'

'And I thought it was your careful kindness. If you said black, I wanted to say white!'

Their laughter mingled and then the flame of passion drove them back into each other's arms. Finally, the champagne poured out and sipped, they sat together on the sofa, wonderingly, eyes meeting eyes with the depth and hunger of loving. They were alone together, wanting each other and aware of the dangers. . .

Nicola could not remove her gaze from his face, nor he from hers. They noticed every shade of expression, their love a miracle.

'When,' she asked hesitantly, 'did you know that you loved me?'

His answer came deep and low. 'At Mark and Charlotte's wedding. I knew, also, that I'd never been in love before, or known its pain.' He looked at her with mounting passion. 'I could not endure the thought of Stuart.'

Her heart thumped. Why hadn't she realised? Why had she been so narrow, so foolish?

She said solemnly, but with a touching honesty, 'I built up my broken engagement, wallowed in it. . .and you were right in everything you said. . . How blind I was——'

Alex could not resist giving a throaty chuckle. 'According to you, *I'm* the blind one!'

She covered her face with her hands and then lowered them slowly as she asked, 'Will you ever forget that I told you I loved you first?' She looked anxious, half pleading.

He held her gaze and said firmly, 'I never want to forget. . . I shall remind you of the fact every day. It is my proudest moment, my darling. And you're superb when you're angry.'

There was a moment of deep silence before he went on, 'That brings me to the most important question. . .' His expression changed to a great tenderness. 'Will you marry me? Just as soon as I can get a special licence?'

Her eyes rounded in surprise at the idea of a special licence, but she said solemnly, her pulse quickening, 'I'll marry you any time, anywhere. . . Oh, *Alex*. . . I'm so much in love with you!'

The words rushed out and he drew her bodily into his arms, looking down at her in adoration. 'And I with you,' he murmured, holding her closer. 'You'll never know what a temptation you've been,' he added tensely, his eyes darkening with a passionate significance.

Nicola shivered with an excitement that was new and all-consuming, her need of him like some vital force within her, as she felt the warmth of his kiss, deep, penetrating. Ecstasy sensitised every part of her body, leaving her trembling with desire, as for a second she drew back and whispered, 'As your wife, may I *always* be your temptation.'

BARBARY WHARF

Will Gina Tyrrell succeed in her plans to oust
Nick Caspian from the Sentinel –
or will Nick fight back?

There is only one way for Nick to win, but it might,
in the end, cost him everything!

The final book in the Barbary Wharf series

SURRENDER

Available from November 1992   Price: £2.99

W●RLDWIDE

*Available from Boots, Martins, John Menzies, W.H. Smith,
most supermarkets and other paperback stockists.
Also available from Mills & Boon Reader Service, PO Box 236,
Thornton Road, Croydon, Surrey CR9 3RU.*

Mills & Boon

Four brand new romances from favourite Mills & Boon authors have been specially selected to make your Christmas special.

THE FINAL SURRENDER
Elizabeth Oldfield

SOMETHING IN RETURN
Karen van der Zee

HABIT OF COMMAND
Sophie Weston

CHARADE OF THE HEART
Cathy Williams

Published in November 1992   Price: £6.80

Available from Boots, Martins, John Menzies, W.H. Smith, most supermarkets and other paperback stockists. Also available from Mills & Boon Reader Service, PO Box 236, Thornton Road, Croydon, Surrey CR9 3RU.

Mills & Boon

—MEDICAL ROMANCE—

The books for enjoyment this month are:

A PERFECT HERO Caroline Anderson
THE HEALING HEART Marion Lennox
DOCTOR'S TEMPTATION Sonia Deane
TOMORROW IS ANOTHER DAY Hazel Fisher

♥ ♥ ♥ ♥ ♥

Treats in store!

Watch next month for the following absorbing stories:

BEYOND HEAVEN AND EARTH Sara Burton
SISTER AT HILLSIDE Clare Lavenham
IN SAFE HANDS Margaret O'Neill
STORM IN PARADISE Judith Worthy

Available from Boots, Martins, John Menzies, W.H. Smith, most supermarkets and other paperback stockists.

Also available from Mills & Boon Reader Service, P.O. Box 236, Thornton Road, Croydon, Surrey CR9 3RU.

Readers in South Africa - write to:
Book Services International Ltd, P.O. Box 41654, Craighall, Transvaal 2024.